A Five-Star Family Reunion

Just in time for Christmas!

The Pearson family promised their late mother that no matter what, they would *always* spend Christmas together. However, it has been three years and their special tradition is almost lost and forgotten...

Chiara has been traveling the world, but she's running out of money and needs help to get home. Meanwhile, Marco has been busy expanding the family hotel business in Europe, and *unexpectedly* expanding the family too. Having insisted his children make it back by Christmas Eve, Joshua has been preparing their Vermont cabin, until the arrival of his beautiful neighbor puts a wrench in the works...

Whatever it takes, the Pearson family *will* spend Christmas together this year!

Find out more in
Chiara and Evan's story
Wearing His Ring till Christmas
by Nina Singh

Marco and Eleanora's story
One-Night Baby to Christmas Proposal
by Susan Meier

and

Joshua and Rebecca's story
Christmas with His Ballerina
by Jessica Gilmore

Available now!

Dear Reader,

It's been twelve years since I started to write seriously, but although I have aged in that time (no mirror in my attic), as a rule my heroes and heroines have stayed somewhere between their midtwenties and midthirties. So, it was a genuine delight to be asked to write characters in their late forties and fifties.

Joshua married young and has two grown-up children. Widowed a decade ago, he has no interest in a new relationship. After all, who can expect true love twice in a lifetime? Meanwhile, Rebecca has spent her life concentrating on rising to the top of a competitive and demanding career, resulting in her marriage becoming a painful casualty. There's no way she's risking her heart again. But when they find themselves neighbors one Christmas in Vermont, both Joshua and Rebecca realize that maybe they deserve second chances after all.

I loved writing these two and exploring all a snow-filled Vermont has to offer. I do hope you enjoy reading about characters who prove you never know when love will strike!

Love,

Jessica

Christmas with His Ballerina

Jessica Gilmore

Special thanks and acknowledgment are given to
Jessica Gilmore for her contribution to
A Five-Star Family Reunion miniseries.

Recycling programs
for this product may
not exist in your area.

ISBN-13: 978-1-335-73689-5

Christmas with His Ballerina

Copyright © 2022 by Harlequin Enterprises ULC

For questions and comments about the quality of this book,
please contact us at CustomerService@Harlequin.com.

Harlequin Enterprises ULC
22 Adelaide St. West, 41st Floor
Toronto, Ontario M5H 4E3, Canada
www.Harlequin.com

Printed in U.S.A.

Incorrigible lover of a happy-ever-after, **Jessica Gilmore** is lucky enough to work for one of London's best-known theaters. Married with one daughter, one fluffy dog and two dog-loathing cats, she can usually be found with her nose in a book. Jessica writes emotional romance with a hint of humor, a splash of sunshine, delicious food—and equally delicious heroes!

Books by Jessica Gilmore

Harlequin Romance

The Princess Sister Swap

Cinderella and the Vicomte
The Princess and the Single Dad

Billion-Dollar Matches

Indonesian Date with the Single Dad

Fairytale Brides

Reawakened by His Christmas Kiss
Bound by the Prince's Baby

Summer Romance with the Italian Tycoon
Mediterranean Fling to Wedding Ring
Winning Back His Runaway Bride
Christmas with His Cinderella

Visit the Author Profile page
at Harlequin.com for more titles.

CHAPTER ONE

'IT'S THANKSGIVING NEXT WEEK, but it's never too early for this Christmas classic,' the announcer said with her usual over-the-top enthusiasm. 'So, turn up the dial and enjoy some festive spirit.'

Joshua Pearson tapped his fingers on the steering wheel as the well-known notes filled his car, humming a little during the verse before segueing into singing the chorus almost on autopilot. But there was no soprano and tenor joining in from the back seat —and it was a long time since a sweet alto had harmonised from the passenger seat. His voice died away. It wasn't the same heading to the Vermont cabin alone. But at least he wouldn't be spending Christmas alone this year, burying himself in work, ensuring other families enjoyed their Christmases while missing his. Because, after three years apart, the Pearson family would be spending Christmas together again.

He glanced at the empty passenger seat. *Almost* all the Pearsons. Joshua swallowed. It had been ten years since Gabriella had died but at times the grief was so raw it felt like yesterday. Christmas was one of those times. Gabriella had loved Christmas—and she would be so happy to know that the kids were coming home this year. *Kids*. Marco was thirty-two and Chiara twenty-seven, but they would always be kids to him. He smiled wryly. And now he sounded like his own father.

The light was beginning to fade, the late autumnal sky low and grey, the drizzle falling on his windscreen turning heavier. It had been too long since he'd driven this route from New York to the Vermont cabin and he had never driven it alone, but if the family were to gather there for Christmas he needed to check everything was in order. No, not just in order, perfect.

As Joshua pulled off the highway onto a tree-lined lane the world changed, farmland rolling off in one direction, mountains framing the distance. How he loved it here, the small picturesque town, the beautiful river, the terrain providing hikes in the spring and summer, skiing in the winter, the perfect contrast to the never-ending bustle of New York. Joshua breathed it all in. This weekend away was a good idea. He couldn't remember the last time he'd taken a break, a trip that wasn't to one of the hotels he ran or a check on his competition. Maybe he needed to make sure he got out into nature while he was here, not spend *all* his time tidying.

As he steered around a sharp bend, he saw a car pulled over by the side of the road up ahead, a woman standing next to it, hands on hips. Nobody else seemed to be around and Joshua braked, pulling in behind the sleek silver vehicle. The woman looked around, her expression mingling hope and wariness. Bundled in a big white coat, she looked to be in her early to mid-forties, blonde hair pulled back in a ponytail. Joshua rolled down his window and stuck his head out.

'Need a hand?'

She half stepped back. 'No, thanks. I've called someone; they should be here any moment.'

'Tyre?'

'No. A light came on and…anyway, someone is coming so please don't let me detain you.'

With a jolt Joshua realised that she was

afraid. Afraid of him. But of course, it was dusk, the road was empty and they were several miles from the nearest town.

'Look,' he said. 'I don't want to make you uncomfortable, but would it be okay if I just waited here until someone turns up? I won't get out my car. But if it was my wife or daughter, I'd want to know they weren't alone.'

The woman bit her lip, clearly indecisive.

'I'm Joshua Pearson,' he added. 'I'm CEO of the Grand York Hotel Group. Our flagship hotel is in Greenwich Village; I don't know if you know it.'

She huddled a little further into her coat. 'I know it.'

'I'm just heading to my cabin. To get ready for Christmas.'

The glimmer of a smile appeared. 'It's not even Thanksgiving.'

'I know, but we haven't been there for some time. It's been three years since we all spent Christmas together so I wanted to make sure everything is okay. Clean and tidy, order food and wood. That kind of thing.'

'I see.' She shivered and wrapped her arms around herself.

'You should get back in your car.'

'The engine won't start so it's just as cold in there. At least out here I can move around.'

'I have a blanket in the back. Do you want it?'

The glimmer of a smile was back. 'A blanket?'

'And a flask of hot coffee. My wife always insisted we prepare for all weather when we drove up here. Old habits die hard. I almost packed snacks for the kids.'

'How old are they?'

'Now? Thirty-two and twenty-seven, but if they *were* here I'd have apple slices and juice just in case.'

The smile widened. 'Thirty-two and twenty-seven?'

'I know, I don't look old enough. I was pretty much a child groom.'

'Right.'

'The blanket? I could put it on the hood and get back in the car?' he offered.

'You must think I'm paranoid.'

'No, I think you're sensible.' Joshua opened his door and jumped out of the car, opening the back door so he could grab the emergency bag that was always within reach. Gabriella had been the impulsive one of the two of them, but she had always been insistent that they never head out in winter without blankets and food, just in case they were caught out by bad weather. As Joshua extracted the blanket and flask, he sent a quick thanks up towards the sky.

'Here.' He held them up. 'Take these.'

As promised, he put the blanket and flask on the hood of his car and climbed back into the driver's seat. Once he'd closed the door the woman stepped forward and retrieved them.

'Thank you. I'm not used to driving alone, or even being out the city. I'll remember this for next time.' She looked towards her car and back at him. 'I'm going to...'

'Absolutely, get in the car and warm up.'

'Thank you again. Tell your wife she is a wise woman.'

He just nodded. She turned and headed back to the car and as Joshua rolled his window back up he took in long, slim, jeans clad legs and the swish of silky blonde hair. He sat back and pulled out his phone, checking his emails, losing himself in work until, with a jolt of surprise, he saw headlights behind him and a van pulling in and remembered where he was. It was almost dark, but he could make out the name of the local garage and recognised the proprietor. Putting his phone away, he turned his own engine on and, with a wave, headed back out towards town and his cabin beyond.

Rebecca moved, trying to escape the slant of sunlight peeking through the curtains, only for the beep of her phone to pull her closer to consciousness as she tried to make out her surroundings. Of course. Despite being just five miles away from her destination, she had ended up staying in the local inn as the garage had been unable to fix her car that evening. Not that she'd seen that much of the inn; cold and tired, she'd asked for soup in her room and then tumbled into bed. She must have slept well because not only had she not woken in the night—unusual for her—but, despite the abrupt awakening, she felt more refreshed than she had for a long, long time. She fumbled for her phone, wincing at the brightness of the light, and answered it.

'Hello?' she half croaked.

'Rebecca? Did I wake you?' There was no doubting the surprise in Anita's voice.

'What time is it?'

'After ten. I have never known you sleep so late.'

Truth be told, Rebecca couldn't remember the last time she had slept so late either.

'Must be the country air,' she said, struggling to sit up.

Her mornings usually began at six. A yoga session followed by a smoothie then into the office at eight for an hour's work before morning class. She still took part in the daily ballet class that had been an integral part of her life for as long as she could remember, but now she went from class back to the office, or to talk to donors or designers or conductors, to watch rehearsals or join planning meetings. But she welcomed that hour and a half when she and the dancers were still as one, muscle memory taking over, her mind focused only on the placement of her foot and arm.

'All recovered from your adventures?' Anita asked.

'I don't know, Anita. Maybe it was a sign.' Rebecca pushed the covers back and clambered out of bed to pull open the curtains. The scene that greeted her was positively bucolic—and alien. The grounds of the inn led to a wide river, beyond which trees, all dark gold and orange as autumn faded to winter, stretched out to the distant mountains, already white topped. She was used to city streets, car horns blaring, constant chatter. The silence and beauty were disconcerting. 'I don't belong here. Maybe I should come back. I don't want Ivan to think he's won.'

There was a long silence at the end of the phone. 'This isn't about Ivan, or your divorce, Rebecca. It's about you not taking a break for four years. What would you say to one of your dancers if they did that?'

Rebecca didn't answer. She knew Anita was right. It wasn't just the gruelling toll that her divorce had taken on her mentally, or the fact that the end of their high-profile marriage was all over the front pages that had made a few weeks away so imperative. It was the fact she had buried herself in work to escape the bitter reality of her failing marriage and hadn't taken as much as a day off in years. But for someone who prided herself on her strength and resilience, for whom perfection was essential, not a goal, it was humiliating to be ordered to take a few weeks off, even if she knew her CEO had done so with the best of intentions.

Just as it was humiliating to have had to be rescued yesterday. She had never played the damsel in distress, not even on stage. She didn't mean to start at the age of forty-eight.

'Look, Rebecca. Let me handle any publicity; it's what you pay me for.' The briskness in Anita's voice had been replaced by the

coaxing tones which helped make her so successful as a publicist. 'You just spend some
time reading and hiking and sleeping and,
before you know it, it will be late December
and Trudie and I will join you for Christmas.'

'I guess, but it still feels like running away.'

'Just try it for a week. If the cabin feels too
remote or rustic, then you can always head to
Europe or the Caribbean for a few weeks...'

'No, remote sounds good.' Anywhere
where people didn't recognise her. And it
was really kind of Anita and Trudie to offer
her their beloved retreat for so long—besides,
knowing her friends, their cabin was bound
to be on the luxurious side of rustic. Anita
was a well-known publicist and agent with
plenty of A-list clients and Trudie a surgeon
and both women enjoyed the finer things in
life. 'I'm looking forward to it.'

'And it's not that remote really,' Anita
reassured her. 'You're just five miles from
Newington and although the cabin isn't over-
looked there are others all around the lake.
It's a pretty sociable place in summer and
at weekends. The Cohens have the cabin on
your right and they usually spend at least two
weekends a month there. The Pearsons are
on your left, but it's been a long time since
Joshua was up...'

Rebecca clutched the phone tighter. 'Joshua Pearson? CEO of the Grand York Hotel Group?'

'You know him?'

'No, but he was the Good Samaritan who waited with me yesterday. In fact I still have his flask and blanket.' It had been getting dark and she hadn't really seen him, just the impression of broad shoulders and the memory of a warm, kind voice.

'That means he *is* up. That's interesting. First time in a long while.'

'Maybe he's just too busy to get away often.'

'Maybe, but that won't be the whole reason. Once they were up whenever they could manage and always at Christmas. But after his wife—Gabriella—died, they used the cabin less and less. He still made an effort to come up for Christmas with the kids but even that stopped eventually. But it sounds like they're reviving the tradition. I'm pleased, they're a nice family. Now, what are your plans for today, or what's left of it?'

'Get dressed, collect the car, do a food shop and settle into the cabin.'

'Perfect. Stay away from your emails, do not Google your name. A proper digital detox, that's what you need.'

'I'll try. Thanks, Anita.'

'Any time. Anything for my best friend and first client. Take care, Bec.'

'And you. Love to Trudie.'

Rebecca put her phone down and leaned against the pillow. So her rescuer of the night before lived just next door? That was good; she could return his items with a thank you gift. She didn't really like being beholden to anyone. Even using Anita's cabin for free made her uncomfortable and she had been friends with Anita since she was fourteen and the two of them had started at the prestigious New York City Ballet Academy. They had been rivals, friends and each other's cheerleaders until Anita had realised at eighteen that her injury-prone knees would never survive a ballet career. Channelling her drive into the agency she started instead, she had represented Rebecca as her career soared. It had been a canny move for both women, Anita as focused and creative in business as she had been on stage. Thanks to her, Rebecca's success on stage had been replicated off stage and that had always been a positive thing—until the headlines of the last few weeks. Now anonymity seemed blissful.

And that was what she was being granted. So no more prevaricating. It was time to get up and find her home for the next few weeks.

It didn't take long for Rebecca to do the bits of shopping she needed to do and to drive the short distance to Anita's cabin. Cabin! A humble word for the impressive architect-designed glass, stone and wood house positioned to make the most of the stunning views over the lake to the mountains beyond. Despite several invitations, Rebecca had never visited before and she explored the luxurious vacation home, feeling the tension melt away. She was going to be very comfortable here.

Downstairs was one huge space for living, dining and cooking, the space designed to showcase the gleaming designer kitchen, vast open fire and floor-to-ceiling windows. The stone floor was warmed by underfloor heating, the expensive leather sofas softened with accent cushions, the walls the same wood and stone as the exterior. Rebecca's guest room had its own bathroom, balcony and reading nook. Exile couldn't be more luxurious.

Once she'd unpacked, she picked up the blanket, washed flask and a box of cinnamon buns she'd bought from the local bakery and, slightly nervously, walked along the lakeside path that connected all the properties.

Joshua Pearson's cabin shared the same spectacular views from its position thirty yards back from the lakeside but that was all the two cabins had in common. His was a much more modest affair, a painted wooden two-storey home with a deck at the back. As she neared, she saw that the paint was faded, the window frames blistering, and the roof looked like it was missing a shingle or two. A ladder was propped up to the roof and as she stepped onto the path leading up to the cabin Joshua Pearson climbed down the ladder, a tool belt around his waist. Rebecca stopped, unaccountably shy, all too aware of strong muscled legs, a very nice backside and the broad shoulders she had noted before. As he turned, she took in brown smiling eyes and slightly messy dark hair peppered with grey at the temples.

'Hi,' she said. 'I hope I'm not disturbing you. I just wanted to return your things from last night.'

'Hi there.' He stepped off the ladder and came towards her. 'Glad to see you safe and sound. Good detective work tracking me down.'

'It wasn't too hard. You gave me your name and, as it turns out, we're neighbours. I'm staying in Anita's house. I'm Rebecca, Rebecca Nelson.'

'Nice to meet you again, Rebecca.' His

forehead crinkled. 'Have we met? You look familiar.'

'I've been to your hotel a few times.'

'That might be it.' He didn't look convinced.

'And you may have seen me dance,' she added reluctantly. So much for anonymity. 'I'm the Artistic Director of the New York City Ballet and I used to be the Principal Ballerina there.'

'Of course, Anita has a photo of you in her hallway. And yes, I have seen you dance. A few times. My wife loved the ballet. She went all the time. To be honest, the first time I went with her I was dreading it, but I really enjoyed it. But it was her thing; I only went when invited. She was a huge fan of yours.'

Rebecca swallowed. *I only went when invited.* Such a simple statement but it spoke volumes. Of respect. If only Ivan had been so accommodating of personal space and preference. 'Well, anyway, I wanted to return your blanket and flask, and I bought you some cinnamon buns from the bakery in town. Anita said they were the best she's ever tasted.'

'There was no need,' he protested. 'I was happy to help, but Anita is right, those buns are spectacular. And perfectly timed. I've got some coffee brewing on the stove. Have you got time for a cup?'

For the first time she could remember Rebecca had nothing but time. 'That would be lovely.'

'Come on in. The cabin is clean at least,' he said ruefully. 'I pay a company to clean the inside and do some yard work, but as you can see the rest of it is in a sorry state. My fault for neglecting it for so long.'

He nodded at an open patio door and after a moment's hesitation Rebecca stepped inside.

Like Anita's cabin, the ground floor was all one room, but that was where the resemblance ended. The simple kitchen with scuffed wooden cabinets took up one end, flanked by a large dining table, bench and chairs. In the middle of the room three battered leather sofas were grouped around the windows to take advantage of the view, and a wall of books covered the other end. The wooden floor looked original, complete with dents and scratches, but the colourful rugs, throws and cushions added warmth and colour, as did the pictures and photos on the walls, mantel and bookshelves.

The room felt homely and cosy. Much loved, despite—or maybe because of—the scuffs and dents and marks.

She put the box of buns and Joshua's things

on the table and took a closer look at the walls. The pictures were a mixture of local scenes and framed children's artwork, but they were vastly outnumbered by the photographs of a laughing, affectionate family, Joshua often at the centre of the group. She recalled Joshua joking that he had been a child groom. It didn't look like he'd been that far from the truth. The fresh-faced bride and groom in the wedding photos barely looked old enough to have graduated high school, let alone got married. She could see twenty years of marriage captured on the wall: the young couple with a tiny baby, then a toddler, then a small child and a second baby. An active family hiking, kayaking, swimming, playing ball, around a Christmas tree, identical smiles on every face—until suddenly there were just three, the smiles forced, shadows in their eyes. Gabriella Pearson had clearly left a huge hole in the heart of her family.

Rebecca had so few photos of her and Ivan: posed wedding photos, the two of them at events, but nothing so carefree or un-staged, and there were few photos from her childhood where she and her sisters looked relaxed. It would have been nice to have been part of a family like this. She bit her lip and turned away; there was no point mourning might-have-beens. She had an amazing career, had been at the top of her profession, was more than solvent. She was luckier than most.

Joshua picked up the blanket and opened a cupboard near the front door and as he did so several items fell out, including ski sticks and an oar, a coat and boots. 'As you can see, it's not just renovating I need to do,' he said. 'Truth is, the place was due a renovation and clear-out a long time ago but after Gabi… Anyway, I thought I could get it ready for Christmas in a weekend, but I vastly underestimated the work needed. I think I'm going to end up staying here from now to Christmas if I want it fit for the holidays.'

Rebecca was aware of a jolt of warmth shooting through her at the realisation Joshua might be next door throughout her stay here. It would certainly make the next few weeks less daunting having someone so capable close by. 'Christmas is a busy time for hotels, isn't it? And the Grand York has always had a reputation for being a real Christmas destination.' A pang of guilt hit her. Christmas was equally important for the ballet world, and she wasn't at the helm of her company where she belonged.

'It is.' He crossed over to the kitchen and opened a cupboard, taking out two plates and mugs. 'But Marco, my son, took over as Managing Director a couple of years ago and every hotel has a very talented manager and team. I'm still CEO but, to be honest, there are times when it feels like a courtesy title.' His smile dimmed. 'It's natural, I guess. The same happened to my father when I took over, and he replaced his father in turn. After thirty years of seven-day weeks and sixteen-hour days they were both happy to spend more time on the golf course, but it turns out I need more than a few board meetings to satisfy me. I know I should be glad Marco is so driven. I *am* glad, although it would be nice if he found time to play sometimes. Anyway, renovating this place is the kind of project I need, something physical and all mine. Come and sit down. Coffee? We may have some herbal tea, but it will be a few years old.'

Rebecca pulled out one of the old Shaker chairs. 'Coffee will be lovely, thanks. What are you thinking of doing?'

'At the very least new window frames, fix the roof, a lick of paint inside and out. Once we had grander plans, before Gabriella...' There it was. The same pause. Even after so many years he clearly missed her very much.

'I don't need fancy windows and a hot tub. But the kitchen is falling apart and the bathrooms could do with replacing. Poor cabin, it doesn't quite compare to Anita's five-star luxury, does it?'

Rebecca accepted the mug filled with strong, aromatic coffee and added some milk from the jug he set in front of her. 'Thank you. Anita's cabin is quite something, true. But this is a home, the kind of place kids can run in straight from the lake dripping water without causing damage. That has a charm of its own that's not to be underestimated. You wouldn't want to lose that.'

His gaze was appraising and she felt it warm her through as he nodded in approval. 'You're right. I don't want to lose the heart of this place, even if the kids *are* grown up. But there's room to make it a little more sophisticated now we're all adults, even if my skills fall short of recreating Anita's palace.'

'This has got lovely bones,' Rebecca said, looking around and appraising, seeing the room as a stage and imagining the choreography of people moving within it. 'I don't think you need to do very much inside. You could probably refresh the kitchen by sanding and revarnishing the cabinets and adding new worktops and appliances. Same in here. New sofas and rugs and fresh paint would make a world of difference. Roofs and windows are beyond my expertise though!'

'The actual DIY doesn't bother me.' He took a seat opposite, long legs sprawled out, strong forearms leaning on the table. He pushed the box of buns towards her. 'Here, help me out. Gabriella and I did this place up from scratch. My uncle left it to me. I thought we should sell it, goodness knows we needed the money with a baby, me in college and Gabi at night school, but she wanted to keep it, to do it up, to have a place where we could let the kids be wild and free in a way city kids can't be.' His laugh was low and reminiscent. 'Neither of us knew what we were doing; it was very trial and error. The first few months we had to camp outside while we gutted it, then we camped inside for longer than I care to remember. Marco was five and Chiara a baby by the time we made it habitable. The sofas, this table, all second-hand, the bathrooms from end of line sales. But along the way I became a decent plumber, joiner and electrician. One thing I don't have though is an eye. We painted it white because that was the cheapest option, but Gabriella loved to bring in swatches and imagine how she might redecorate when she had the time. I have to admit, the thought of that gives me nightmares. I may need to just give it a fresh coat of white.'

Rebecca took another sip of her coffee, her mind racing. She didn't want to intrude, but he clearly needed help—and she had the time. 'Look, I'm no expert but I think I have a decent eye, a lifetime of costumes and backdrops has seen to that, and I am a pretty dab hand with a paintbrush. I'm here until Christmas myself with no plans, so if you need a hand—or someone to consult on colour— just ask.'

'You're here till Christmas?'

'Long story,' she said briefly, looking down to escape his keen gaze. To her surprise, her plate was empty, with just a few crumbs left on it. She barely remembered taking the bun, let alone eating it. 'I better go and get settled in. But it's a genuine offer. If you want any help, just ask.'

'I will. Thanks for the treats. See you around, neighbour.'

Rebecca said her own goodbyes and as she left the cabin was aware of a spring in her step. It was good to know she had a friendly face so close, and even better to have the possibility of something to do rather than sit and dwell on the failure of her marriage. Her pleasure in the realisation had nothing to do with a pair of twinkling brown eyes and fine shoulders. After the failure of her marriage, the last thing she wanted to do was dip back into the dating pool. But friendly neighbours? Well, that sounded about perfect.

CHAPTER TWO

JOSHUA PULLED UP in front of next door's gate and killed the engine, still indecisive. Had Rebecca meant it when she had offered to help him decorate, or was she just being polite?

It wasn't the only question that had kept him occupied over the weekend. He couldn't help wondering what a woman like Rebecca was doing rusticating alone in Vermont for five weeks. She had an important job; could they spare her for so long?

Well, if she wanted to tell him she would. Maybe she'd been ill and was recuperating. There were deep shadows under her hazel eyes that looked like they had been there some time, and a reserve in her manner that hinted at secrets.

Or a woman who just liked her privacy.

But after forty-eight hours of his own company, excepting only a brief video call with Marco to show him all the work that needed to be done, Joshua was willing to risk a rebuff. He didn't need other people around him constantly, but some occasional conversation with another person would be nice.

He jumped out of the car and walked down the path to the cabin. It was impressive even from the outside, the grounds landscaped to look natural and blend in with the surroundings, only more so, the cabin the same with its blend of walls of glass and stone, wood an accent. It wasn't really a cabin at all, it was a luxury house pretending and, for all its impressiveness, he secretly preferred his own painted wooden house, renovated with love and laughter.

Joshua knocked on the door and stood back, and after a moment the door half opened and Rebecca peeked out. He could see her visibly relax when she recognised him and the door closed again, he heard a chain released and she opened it fully.

'Sorry to disturb you.'

'No, not at all. I just wasn't expecting anyone.' But she looked as fresh and ready as if she had been expecting a house load of visitors. Her hair was pulled back into the same shining ponytail she'd worn on the previous two occasions they had met, her face discreetly but perfectly made up, and she wore well-tailored grey trousers with a blue silk blouse and something that was either a cardigan or a jacket or something in between in a grey-blue tweed. Diamond studs sparkled discreetly in shapely ears. Was she going somewhere?

'I would have called first, but I don't actually have your number.' He could have asked Anita, he supposed, but it seemed silly to bother her when Rebecca was just next door.

And a single man asking for a possibly single woman's number provoked speculation, the kind of speculation he liked to avoid. He hadn't dated since Gabriella's death and he had no intention of starting to do so, no matter what friends and relatives said.

He'd had perfection and it was unlikely he'd be lucky enough to find it again. How could he settle for less?

But the raw rasp of pain, the instant revulsion that for so long had hit him whenever anyone, however well meaning, suggested he *'get back out there'* was missing. When had that happened?

'You should probably have it, and I yours. After all, we are neighbours.' She stood back. 'Do you want to come in?'

Joshua stepped back. She was clearly busy. 'I don't want to delay you.'

'Delay me?'

'Are you about to head out?' He gestured at her outfit and, as she looked down, pink crept over her cheekbones.

'I do look like I'm about to chair a meeting, don't I? The problem is I only have three types of outfits. Workout clothes, work clothes and occasion wear, the costumes I need for my life. I don't have casual wear because I don't usually have unscheduled time. I suppose I could have worn leggings and a hoodie, but...' She shook her head briskly. 'I'm babbling. Do come in.'

Joshua kicked his boots off before entering the cabin. It was a few years since he'd last been over to Anita and Trudie's for Christmas drinks, but the interior was as gleaming and luxurious as he remembered. The walls were mostly glass or exposed stone. Where they were painted, they were various shades of grey or taupe, with brighter accent colours picked up by the exquisite ornaments and expensive-looking cushions on the even more expensive-looking sofas. Definitely not a place where a child would be welcome to run in dripping wet, he thought, remembering Rebecca's perceptive comment about his own home.

A laptop sat open on the coffee table, and

on the screen he could see people stretching in seemingly impossible ways. Rebecca followed his glance and sighed. 'Stepping away isn't easy in my job. My assistant is filtering my emails but I have managed to get her to agree to send me the most important and I insisted on watching class at least. It's not the same online but at least I can send notes and think about casting.'

'In that case, maybe I have the perfect distraction. And maybe the answer to your wardrobe issues' He was right; there was a mystery about her prolonged stay here. She didn't seem to have any vacation plans or want to switch off from her work.

She raised a querying eyebrow.

'I'm heading into the city and was going to ask if you needed anything. The temperature has dropped and although I don't think snow is imminent it could be here soon. If you need to stock up then now is your opportunity. But I'm equally happy to give you a lift or to take orders.'

'The city?'

'Temper your expectations,' he warned her. 'To you it may look more like a small town. Fifteen thousand inhabitants, if that, but they have some good hardware stores and I need supplies, some decent clothing places and some outdoor activity suppliers. It's no New York but it does for what I need.'

'Sounds great. I'd love a lift if that's okay?'

'Of course.'

She looked quickly over to the laptop and hesitated, clearly drawn to the movement on screen. 'Just give me five. I'll be right with you.'

It felt strangely intimate with Rebecca sitting in the passenger seat next to him as Joshua drove the fifteen miles to the nearest city. She had a still, compelling presence and, although she didn't say much, he was all too aware of her, of long, lean elegant legs, her perfume.

It's okay, he could hear Gabi saying, her rich laugh pealing out. *You're allowed to find her attractive. She is attractive.*

'The stores I need are on the outskirts of town,' he said as they got nearer to the city boundary. 'But there's a popular shopping village close by. I could drop you there if you wanted or if you don't mind waiting there are plenty more stores in the centre.'

'What are your chores?'

'I need to get some more wood, tools, nails…everything really.' Joshua blew out a breath. 'I want to get the roof and windows done this week and do at least one layer of weatherproofing paint so that when the snow comes I can concentrate on inside. Late November is not the best time to be starting this kind of job—time is definitely not on my side! Then I have the measurements for the kitchen worktop and quantities of tiles I need. The bathroom fittings themselves are fine, but they could do with a retile, new taps and floors. If I get everything ordered and delivered this week then it doesn't matter when the snow comes. I'll have plenty to occupy myself with.'

'I'm happy to come with you, if you don't mind the company.'

'Not at all.'

In fact Joshua was glad of her company because although ordering the wood, tools, outside paint and varnish he needed was no problem at all, he found himself stuck when it came to the tiles, interior paint and kitchen worktops and handles. 'There are so many shades of grey,' he said. 'Why is it so popular? If I get it wrong, I'll be giving the cabin a prison chic look, and that's not what I'm going for.'

Rebecca laughed and he couldn't help but note how musical the sound was. 'Your hotels are a byword for comfort mixed with luxury.

You can't be as ignorant about colour and texture as you claim.'

'I hire people,' he said. 'The hotels employ some very talented designers. They give me mood boards and I usually agree.' It wasn't quite as clear-cut as he was making out. He had strong views on everything that went into his hotels, from the quality of the bed linen to the toiletries to the décor in the bar, but he was stuck when it came to the cabin. Maybe because it was the last piece of Gabriella. After all, he had moved out of the family house to an apartment after the kids had left home, changed the car, started to wear his hair shorter, bought new clothes. The cabin was the only thing that was exactly the same as it had been when she'd died, and although he knew it needed a refresh and she would want him to do it, making a decision almost paralysed him.

'In that case, let's make our own mood boards before you choose,' she said. 'I owe you lunch as a thank you for thinking to ask me to come along today, so we can discuss exactly what you have in mind then and come back. Better to get it right.'

Joshua protested that she didn't owe him anything, but she was insistent and so, after paying for his order and arranging delivery for later that day, he drove them into the centre of the small city. It was, as he had warned her, tiny although it held the county municipal buildings. The city dated back a couple of hundred years and was attractive, with parks and heritage buildings, a wide river and the nearby mountains creating a dramatic backdrop. The shops included a few chains and a lot of independents, including coffee shops, bookshops and enough clothes shops for Rebecca to diversify and snow-proof her wardrobe. Joshua dropped her off, arranging to meet her at a popular riverside restaurant in a couple of hours' time, before heading off to park and do his own bits and pieces.

It should have been odd, doing something as personal as shopping for mundane DIY items with a near stranger, but somehow it had felt natural. Rebecca had seemed genuinely interested, asking questions about why he wanted certain tools, chipping in with details about building sets, which was clearly a much more intricate business than Joshua had realised. It was amazing how much she had to be involved in, lighting and costume and set as important as the dance itself—to say nothing of the commercial concerns.

Not that dissimilar to running a hotel chain!

In fact, mood boards or no mood boards,

Joshua was looking forward to lunch, and to getting to know his mysterious neighbour better.

Small though the city centre might be, it had everything Rebecca needed and by the time she met up with Joshua she was lugging an obscene number of bags containing jeans, jumpers, tops and cardigans, flat winter boots plus winter walking boots and socks and some base layers. New York could get extremely cold, so she wasn't completely ill equipped, but they had passed some enticing-looking trails as they drove and she realised how much she wanted to get out in the fresh if chilly country air. She relinquished her bags to the hostess with no small relief before she was escorted through the restaurant to the glassed-in terrace overlooking the river where Joshua sat reading through a menu.

She hesitated, momentarily and unaccountably shy. He seemed so in control, so relaxed, as much at home in this upmarket restaurant as he had been in the hardware store. She was aware of the hostess sneaking an approving look at him and was surprised by a jolt of something that felt very much like jealousy. Which was ridiculous. She barely knew him, and the last thing Rebecca was interested in was any kind of relationship.

She'd been living fully apart from Ivan for two years now, but the divorce had been so drawn out, so difficult, so vicious that she hadn't felt free until she'd received her decree. And even then he'd managed to ensure she couldn't wholly escape him, briefing against her, their names coupled in headlines dissecting just why their marriage had finished, the blame squarely targeted at her.

'Success?' Joshua asked as she took her seat and accepted the menu from the hostess with a smile.

'I think so,' she said cautiously. 'The only thing I haven't thought through is food supplies. Do the roads get impassable?'

'Not the main roads, but I have had to dig out the track to the cabin before. I would do a basics—and plenty of them—grocery shop sooner rather than later, but the snowploughs are pretty good; you wouldn't find yourself gnawing on the last bit of hard biscuit for too long.'

'In that case I will get stocked up—and make sure I eat well now.' Rebecca scanned the menu. 'The Thanksgiving special looks amazing, although I can't believe it's Thanksgiving this week.'

'Do you have plans?'

'For Thanksgiving? I usually work.' It wasn't really an answer, and she could see him acknowledge the deflection. 'You?'

'I usually work too, but this year I am planning a turkey sub, a large slab of pumpkin pie and a long hike. Nowhere better to feel thankful than amongst the elements.'

'That sounds perfect.' And it did. Much better than sitting in alone and trying not to think about burying herself in work. Ivan had accused her of not being able to think about anything else; it would be ironic if this time away proved his point. 'I could go back to New York…' She didn't want Joshua to think she didn't have *any* options. 'But I think I'd find it hard to come back if I did. And I've bought all these clothes now.'

'Not enjoying your vacation?' There was no judgement in his tone or in the kind, dark eyes, just interest and a tinge of concern.

'It's not that. I'm just not used to having any leisure time. I feel guilty if I'm not doing something.'

'You can take a good work ethic too far. But I am willing to take advantage of your need to be busy. If you meant that offer to help…'

'I did!'

'Then, as you have probably grasped, I have bitten off rather a huge slab of project and I only have just over a month to complete it. Any help would be greatly appreciated. And in return...' His eyes darkened and a hint of a smile twisted his mouth. To her surprise—and alarm—Rebecca felt her stomach twinge with something that felt very like desire.

It was a relief when at that moment the waitress came over for their orders. Joshua gestured for Rebecca to go first, and she opted for the Thanksgiving special of spiced pumpkin soup, turkey with all the trimmings and pecan pie with a glass of white wine.

'I *am* on holiday,' she said, almost defensively. Too many people were prurient about dancers' diets, assuming they existed on cotton wool or threw their food up. 'And my actual Thanksgiving meal is more likely to be pasta and salad. I might as well go for it now.'

'That's an excellent idea. I'll have the same, and a non-alcoholic beer,' Joshua told the waitress. He leaned back and smiled over at Rebecca, a slow, approving smile which lit her up inside like it was July Fourth not Thanksgiving. 'Good choice. Looks like this partnership is already paying dividends.'

'Partnership?'

'That's what I was about to propose. You help me and I help you.'

'Intriguing.' She held his gaze, on the surface as cool and collected as ever. 'Tell me more.'

'You want to keep busy, and I clearly need an assistant if I want to get everything done on time, but you are on vacation. So my suggestion is that I pay you…'

'I don't need paying!'

His smile widened. 'Pay you by showing you what a fantastic place Vermont is to holiday in, starting with an invitation to join me on my Thanksgiving hike. What do you say?'

'You're sure I wouldn't be intruding?'

'Not at all.'

She sat back as the waitress brought her wine and Joshua's beer to the table, her mind racing. If she accepted his proposal then she would have a structure and purpose to her time away, something she knew she needed. But she would also be spending a great deal of time with Joshua Pearson. On one hand that was no bad thing as he was undeniably attractive, not just on the outside but he seemed to have a good heart as well. But she had a track record of choosing badly and was in no state to get into another relationship — if one was even on the cards.

And as usual she was overthinking things.

'Deal,' she said quickly, before she could talk herself out of it. 'I'm in. Which means we need to get started on those mood boards. Tell me your feelings about blue.'

CHAPTER THREE

ONCE HE'D DROPPED Rebecca and her bags back at her cabin, Joshua started to regret the impulse that had led him to invite her along on his Thanksgiving hike. He barely knew her—and the day they had spent together confirmed his suspicion that she was the type to keep her cards close to her chest. He didn't even know if she was in a relationship, although he had noted that her left hand was ring free.

He had also noticed that her smile was rare but lit up her whole face, her laugh at times croaky and infectious, at odds with her melodic voice, at other times like music, that every gesture was imbued with an unconscious grace bred into every line.

And that he wanted to know all about her.

Another reason this hike—and the exchange of outings for work—was such a bad idea. But he couldn't back out of either now. Especially not after she had patiently and methodically gone through every room with him so that he had been able to return to the shop with a clearer idea of what he wanted, her suggestions insightful and sometimes inspired.

Joshua looked over at the wall, at all the photos of his beloved, vivacious, impulsive wife. Gabriella wouldn't have hesitated to invite Rebecca along. But he couldn't help feeling that the attraction he felt for Rebecca was a betrayal of his wife.

He also knew that she would tell him not to be so ridiculous. That she would want him to enjoy both life and company.

'I miss you,' he said softly and for a moment the air stilled as if she were there.

By the time Thanksgiving dawned bright and cold and, more importantly, dry, Joshua felt much easier about spending time with Rebecca. She'd spent a good ten hours over the last two days, sanding the kitchen cabinets inside and out. There hadn't been much opportunity to speak as he'd been too busy on the roof and windows, but they had shared a companionable afternoon snack. Both days he'd been on the verge of inviting her for dinner—and both days she had paused before saying goodbye as if she had something to say, but neither had extended any kind of invitation. Although it did seem ridiculous when they were both spending the evening in solitary splendour.

As agreed, Joshua swung by for Rebecca early. She was ready and waiting for him in dark walking trousers, a red sweater and her white coat, a rucksack at her feet. Somehow, she made the practical outfit look like couture, her simply pulled back hair like an expensive style.

'I baked,' she announced as she opened the door. 'Fruit and nut flapjacks. To be honest they're the only thing I know how to bake, but they are instant energy providers. You're not allergic, are you?'

'Not at all; they sound great. Shall we get going?'

He'd arranged to collect their picnic from a local café so made a quick detour to the town then, after firmly refusing Rebecca's offer to pay, began the familiar short drive towards the mountains.

Rebecca let out a contented-sounding sigh. 'I'm really looking forward to today. I've not done much hiking, but I've enjoyed what I have done.'

'In a couple of weeks these trails will be covered in snow, so it's good to get out while we can. But the ski slopes here are excellent. Do you ski?'

'Never learned. Never been allowed—a ski injury could ruin a dancer's career.'

'It's not too late.'

'Maybe I'll give it a go.' She paused and looked out of the window. 'I have an inbuilt fear of anything that might cause injury. A dancer's body is her tool—or his tool—and one torn ligament in the wrong place could mean months out, a slow recovery, opportunities missed. It can limit what we're willing to try. It feels strange to know that so many more activities are now open to me.'

'Do you still dance?'

'Morning class only, but I do that every day. I'm missing today's so I added some barre exercises after my morning yoga, using the kitchen worktops as an impromptu barre.'

'This morning? That's active. We have got a long day ahead, you know!'

Rebecca laughed at his evident surprise. 'Morning class is as important to me as coffee is to other people. It wakes up my body and my mind. You should try it.'

'Will you teach me?' Joshua hadn't meant the words to sound suggestive but somehow they did and as soon as he said them he wanted to recall them. But when he looked over at Rebecca her grin had widened.

'If you are very good.'

'I don't own any tights.'

'I'm sure I could lend you some.'

It was Joshua's turn to laugh. 'Now that would be a sight!'

They lapsed back into silence for the rest of the drive, but it was a comfortable silence. Companionable.

In no time at all Joshua had pulled into the car park which marked the beginning of the trail and started to transfer the picnic to his rucksack, despite Rebecca's protestation that she could carry her fair share. He'd chosen the route with care, as they needed to get back before sunset and he knew that Rebecca, although clearly incredibly physically fit, wasn't used to hiking. It was a circular route that took a meandering path to a mountain shelf, which boasted a famous waterfall, followed by a woodland section before they began their descent.

'Got water?' he asked as he locked the car.

She nodded. 'Two bottles.'

'A first aid kit?'

'Yes, sir.'

'Whistle and compass?'

'Check?'

'Bear spray.'

'Won't they be hibernating?'

'Moose spray?'

She looked at him suspiciously but he kept his face smooth. 'It never hurts to be prepared.'

'If I see a moose, I shall just walk around it,' she informed him as she swung the rucksack onto her shoulders with a deft graceful swing and started towards the wooden post that signified the beginning of the trail. Joshua allowed himself a moment to watch her balletic, confident gait, ponytail bobbing jauntily, before breaking into a long stride and catching her up.

They didn't speak much as they started the hike. It was the first time in several years that Joshua had been out in the wild like this and as he took in the almost bare trees, the blue sky and breathed in the fresh, cold air, so pure it almost hurt his city lungs, he couldn't help thinking about past hikes and trips to the cabin. He felt no different to that young man who had first walked this trail with a baby strapped to his back, yet here he was, over fifty—just—with two adult children. It seemed impossible. For a moment he could see the young man he had been, Gabi at his side, the children running in front, and nostalgia and loss hit him all over again. He'd not been back to this trail since Gabi had died, one of many places he hadn't been able to bear revisiting without her. But it felt right to be here, painful as every step of moving on was.

Rebecca looked equally contemplative as she walked, yet once again the silence was companionable.

After a while the gentle incline became steeper, and Joshua could feel a slight pull in his legs and chest until he slowed the pace. Beside him, Rebecca was barely breathing any harder, although she had unzipped her coat. 'Getting tired?' she asked as she slowed to match him.

'Just pacing myself,' he admitted. 'I go to the gym, play tennis and racquetball, but I'm out of practice on this type of exercise and we've got a long way to go yet. But look at you; you look like you could jog to the top!'

'Dancers have to be incredibly fit. Have you ever done thirty-two fouettés?'

'I can't say I have. Maybe after you've given me a lesson?'

'Let's start with the basics,' she suggested. She lapsed into silence again as they scrabbled up a steep bit and then said, 'Thank you. For inviting me along.'

'You're more than welcome. I needed a

pace setter. I'd forgotten how steep this trail can be in parts.'

'Yes, it hardly feels like you're climbing at times, but when you do you know it! It's beautiful here. Is this a favourite walk?'

'It is, although it's a long time since I last walked it. It was a good one for the kids. Not too steep for most of the ascent, lots of interest. There's a waterfall with a pond that you can swim in in summer, although it's never warmer than absolutely freezing, and a wood with trees to climb.' Every step was a memory. But the pain had eased with every step until he realised with some surprise that he was enjoying himself.

'Then I am doubly grateful you brought me along.' Another pause. 'Is this how you used to spend Thanksgiving? Out here?'

'No, this is the first time. Thanksgiving in the past was a lot more traditional. I used to work the first part of the day then meet up with Gabriella and the kids at her parents'. She was part of a large Italian family so, as you can imagine, there was a lot of laughter and talk and more food than an entire street could eat. They carried on hosting us after she died, and we carried on going, but it was never the same. Once Chiara started travelling, I found a reason to stay at work for most of the day. This is new.'

'Then I'm honoured you asked me to join you.'

'And I'm honoured you accepted.' And he meant it. 'You usually work Thanksgiving too, you said?'

'The show must go on. And it is. Going on.' Her voice faltered for a moment. 'We don't launch *The Nutcracker* for a few more weeks. It premieres Christmas Eve, so rehearsals are ramping up, plus we are starting rehearsals for the productions that will replace it—and then there are the actual performances. We currently have a new contemporary piece alternating with *Giselle* so there are corrections, rehearsals, extra sessions for people in new roles, and of course the shows themselves, sometimes twice a day.'

'You must work eighteen-hour days.'

'Seven days a week sometimes.'

'And I thought the hotel business was demanding.'

'You can't see it as a job.' Her voice turned soft, wistful. 'It's what pays the bills, true, but it's also a way of life. If you start to resent the hours, the physical demands, the emotional demands, then it's time to quit. Some dancers train all their lives, to walk away at the start of their careers. Maybe, like Anita, they realise their bodies just won't sustain them, maybe they realise they like other aspects of ballet—teaching or making costumes or the admin side—or they walk away altogether. But every dancer is all the richer for those hours in the studio, the discipline and beauty we learn.'

Joshua almost envied the love and longing in her voice. He had been brought up to take over the hotels, had worked hard and independently to do so not just competently but to grow and expand his inheritance. Each generation grew the business, from his grandfather's founding of the New York original to his father's expansion into neighbouring buildings, making the Grand York *the* go-to hotel in Greenwich Village. Joshua had opened sister hotels in Boston and Washington—and made the brand synonymous with family-friendly luxury and style.

Now Marco was expanding into Europe, hence his trip to Rome, where they had just recently opened their first Italian hotel. The hotel business was all he knew, and he enjoyed his work, but he had never had the kind of vocation Rebecca clearly had.

'Is ballet what you always wanted to do? When did you start?'

'My mother was a pageant queen,' Rebecca said, quickening her pace again as they reached a less steep incline. 'And when she had me, she wanted to relive her glory days. I was lisping my way through a routine before I was three. She sent me to ballet to help with my poise, but instead stepping into that studio was like coming home.' Her smile was soft and reminiscent. 'By eight I had a scholarship at a local academy and quit the pageant world, but that was okay; I had two younger sisters waiting to step into my heels.'

Joshua eyed the poised, elegant woman beside him. It was hard to see her in the glitzy, over-the-top world of pageants.

'Did your mother mind you stopping?'

Rebecca didn't answer for a while, and the hazel eyes momentarily clouded. 'She didn't understand why. To her, pageants were everything and I think she felt that by rejecting them I was rejecting her. That rather than spending time with her on costumes and hair and routines I wanted to spend time with my ballet teachers. She found—finds—ballet boring. I guess if my dance school had gone in for competitions she might have felt differently, but it was an old-fashioned training establishment. But I loved it, the routine, the striving for perfection. In the end we had less and less to say to each other, then, when I was fourteen, I moved to the city to join the Academy and train full-time. I joined the company at sixteen and life has been full ever since. There's no big feud or anything; we're just not close.'

Joshua tried to imagine disapproving of his children's choices so much he distanced himself from them. It was unimaginable. Sure, he wished Marco would slow down, allow some fun into his life, be a little less driven, but he understood. He knew what it was like to inherit a family legacy, to want to add to it. Whereas with Chiara he wished the opposite. That she would start to settle a little. He knew she was living her mother's unrealised dream by travelling the world, but she had been flitting from job to job and place to place for years. He'd even had to wire her the money to come home for Christmas. Not that he minded at all, but he couldn't help but worry about her future. But they were their choices, and his job was to support them. 'Do you see much of your family now?'

'Not really. My father used to come and watch me several times a year, my mother and sisters occasionally, but my sisters married young and stayed close to home; their daughters are now on the pageant scene. Like I said, I'm not estranged from them or anything dramatic like that, but we occupy different worlds and have for a long time.' She sighed. 'I was made principal when I debuted as Odette/Odile. I was nineteen, less than three years out of the Academy, the youngest principal in the history of the New York City Ballet, a record I still hold. It's a cliché maybe, but the truth is debuting in that role is one of the greatest achievements of a dancer's life. My mother missed it because my younger sister was in a local pageant. It's just how things were, how they are. The company became my family, is my family.'

She had mentioned no significant other, no children.

'The hotel can feel like that,' he said. 'I grew up in it and my children were practically raised there. When Chiara went off travelling and Marco had moved out it was a sanctuary. It still can be. Easier to put in long days there than face my empty apartment.'

'I know exactly what you mean.' And he sensed she really did.

'Which makes it harder giving Marco the freedom to grow and put his stamp on the business. I'm barely fifty. I'm not ready for the golf course yet, if ever.'

'Once upon a time ballerinas retired young. Of course, some still do, but others go on until forty or later, thanks to advances in nutrition and training. But, even with all those advances, it's not a career for life and we all know there's an end point. I was terrified of reaching that point, of having to figure out who I was if I wasn't a dancer. The opportunity to also learn how to manage the company was a lifesaver to me. A year later I was appointed Artistic Director.'

'I'm already CEO. I'm not sure where else to go.'

She laughed. 'True, but maybe there's another opportunity, a different path you haven't seen yet? My life is still in dance, but very different to being a dancer. I've moved on but kept being involved in what I love.'

'Maybe I could turn the cabin into a B&B,' he joked, and she laughed again.

'I'm not sure my sanding skills are of a professional standard.'

It had been one of the freest and most honest conversations Joshua could remember in a long time. What was it about this woman that made opening up so easy? He had no idea, but it was nice to be himself, Joshua Pearson. Not a CEO, not a widower, not a parent. Just a man.

They spent the rest of the morning hiking to the broad mountain shelf, where they stopped to consume turkey subs and pumpkin pie. Rebecca couldn't remember ever feeling so hungry or food tasting so good, the combination of the fresh air, exercise and stunning view all contributing. 'Even with the trees almost bare and no green it's beautiful,' she said dreamily. 'It must be gorgeous in summer.'

'It is. Here.' Joshua handed her a glass. 'Just a mouthful of wine, hiking and alcohol don't mix, but I think we need to toast the moment. To give thanks.'

'Agreed.' She looked at the deep red liquid then back out at the view. 'I'm thankful to be here, for nature. For new friends.' Their eyes met and held. 'And for freedom...' she added almost to herself.

'I am also thankful to be here and for new friends, especially new friends who are handy with a sander. For my children. For the memories I was lucky enough to make, and for being able to recall them with joy not pain.

And for time, the great healer.' It was his turn to speak softly.

'To new friends and renovations.' She held her glass up to him and he mirrored her.

The walk along the mountain shelf was easy, giving Rebecca every opportunity to admire the waterfall and enjoy the winding forest path. It seemed no time at all until they were on the downward path, although the low sun indicated they were well into the afternoon.

'This is exactly what I needed,' she said as they paused at yet another viewpoint. She pulled out her phone to take a picture and put it away without checking her emails. 'This and helping you out. I'm not made to do nothing, but I can see that I did need a break from my routine. I actually managed to sleep over six hours in a row last night.'

Joshua didn't reply, but his glance was understanding and warmed her through.

'It's hard to know when you're close to the edge,' she continued. 'My solution was more hours, more work. Stepping away felt like failure. But more of this and I can see I'll return stronger.'

'It can get like that. I was the same after Gabriella died. I had this urge to be the perfect dad, to be at every school event for Chiara, to be there for Marco at every turn, which was probably stifling for them, to have home-made dinners on the table every night and the laundry basket empty while pulling insane shifts at the hotel. I'd even stand in if we were short a waiter or sou chef. I just didn't want to stop.'

'I felt I had so much to prove, stepping up into such a huge role. I was barely into my mid-forties, a woman, no business experience. It's usual for artistic directors to be dancers, and I had done a business diploma, but nothing could really prepare me for the moment I realised it was all down to me— the rep, the schedule, the hires, the promotions, the wellbeing of the company, commissioning of works and, of course, financial viability. I knew some people thought I would fail. Wanted me to fail.'

'Jealous rivals?'

'No, that's less rife than folklore would have you believe. In the main, dancers are a supportive bunch. In fact, mentoring other dancers is one of the things that brings me the greatest joy. Seeing the youngest dancers shine, helping them find the confidence to do so is so rewarding. I'm old enough to be their mother, and I do see them as my flock of ducklings, ready to be turned into swans.' She hesitated. She didn't really want to ruin such a lovely afternoon by mentioning Ivan, but Joshua had been so open with her she didn't want to dissemble. 'My ex-husband and I had very different ideas about what life after dance should look like. He thought I should join him in LA, raise kids, support his career, maybe join some boards and attend fundraising events. He didn't understand my drive to keep working.'

'Hence the ex?'

She nodded. 'The divorce was finalised last month. It's been tough. He wanted to punish me, I think, for not being who he wanted me to be. Fought my attorneys every step of the way, even though I wanted nothing from him except what was mine to start with. Then, not content with that, he's been briefing against me. Wants to make it clear the divorce is my fault, that I didn't keep my word, that I'm a career mad workaholic.' She laughed, aware the sound was harsh. 'As if that's news! But in the end it got too much. That's why I had to leave New York, to get away from the press interest. And because, thanks to all of it, the stress finally caught up with me.'

'I'm sorry you had to go through that.'

She shrugged. 'It's not the same as losing a wife.'

'You did lose someone—the man you

thought he was. You must have married him hoping for a very different outcome. You are allowed to grieve for what wasn't, Rebecca, whatever form that grief takes. And if it's anger and you want to take that anger out on my floorboards then be my guest!'

Laughing at a joke about her divorce had seemed impossible just a few days ago and yet here she was.

'I'll do that. Thank you.'

'For asking you to sand floorboards? You're welcome.'

'No,' she said. 'For listening. For understanding.'

For a moment Rebecca worried that she'd said too much, revealed too much, but Joshua's insightful comments went some way to assuaging the hurt and guilt she carried. She *was* grieving, she realised. Grieving for the hopeful woman who had stood in a cloud of orange blossom and made vows she had believed were for ever. Grieving for the Ivan she had fallen for, the charming, attentive man who had told her she was perfection—before he had tried to change her. Or maybe she had changed on her own. Maybe he too was grieving and that was why he had lashed out so brutally.

They were almost back at the car park now,

the sun a low ball in the sky and, despite her aching muscles, she felt lighter and freer than she had for many months. She needed to forgive herself as well as Ivan and, thanks to Joshua, she was almost there.

The journey back to the cabins was almost as quiet as the journey there, but again the silence was comfortable, that of friends who were content to be at ease in silence. Joshua drew up outside Anita's and, before Rebecca could assure him she didn't need help, had jumped out of the car and walked around to open her door, extending a hand to help her out.

'Thank you,' she said.

'I was glad of the company. I should thank you.'

'Not just for the day out, although I loved it, but for listening. For helping me put my feelings into perspective. It's going to take some time for me to come to terms with the last couple of years and months, but for the first time I can see it's possible.'

'Grief isn't linear,' he said, his brown eyes darkening with remembered pain. 'I spent a lot of time jumping between the stages and even now I'll find myself angry for a moment that we didn't get to do all the things we planned, but those moments are more and more fleeting. Yours will be too.' He hesitated, then leaned in and kissed her cheek, sweet, chaste and brief, before stepping back. 'Happy Thanksgiving.'

'Happy Thanksgiving,' she echoed, and in a daze watched him return to the car and drive off, one hand lifted in a wave. Then, and only then, she allowed herself to touch the spot on her cheek where he had kissed her.

CHAPTER FOUR

'OKAY, DON'T LOOK! Eyes closed!'

Rebecca's excitement was infectious, and Joshua's grin widened as he obediently kept his eyes closed and allowed her to guide him over the threshold. 'Okay, you can look.'

He opened his eyes and turned, slightly staggered by the transformation she had wrought.

He and Rebecca had decided to concentrate on the first floor to start with and now the window frames were sanded and varnished inside and out, the roof patched and re-shingled and the outside repainted, Joshua was free to concentrate on the two bathrooms while Rebecca had taken over the bedrooms. Paint had been delivered the week before and she had also put together a large order of bed linens and accessories.

'What do you think?' she asked nervously.

He circled round once again. 'I think you're a miracle worker.'

She flushed a rosy pink. 'It's just paint.'
'No, it's more than that.'

She'd started off sanding and varnishing the floors, a job which had taken the best part of a week, and they now shone a warm honey, the colour matched by the window frames. The room itself, Marco's room, was south-facing so she'd picked a light navy for the walls. The bed was made up with white linen, a quilt in various shades of blue the perfect accent, a rug, cushions and curtains matching the lightest shade of the quilt. New lamps sat on the chest of drawers and bedside table and she'd picked a couple of landscapes from downstairs for the walls.

Joshua walked across to the chest of drawers and picked up a newly framed photo, a small Marco standing in his mother's arms. Both Gabriella and their son were laughing, the light golden behind them. He swallowed, his heart full, touched by her thoughtfulness.

He looked at the photograph, remembering Gabriella in dungarees, hair tied back in a scarf, applying white paint to the newly plastered walls, singing along loudly to the radio. The plans she had had for this much-loved place and never fulfilled... He swallowed hard. He knew she would approve of the changes, would tell him they were long overdue, but each change took him further from her.

'Have I overextended the brief?' Rebecca sounded nervous. 'You did say to go crazy with your credit card.'

'No, not at all. This is perfect.' The scruffy room which had housed a child and teen was now a room ready for an adult. It was long past time for the transformation.

'I've almost finished Chiara's room as well.' She pulled him across the landing, her touch soft, and yet it seared him. 'I wasn't sure about yellow, but it works so well. It really brightens up what was quite a gloomy room once morning passed.'

In many ways the room was a match for Marco's, complete with white bed linen and a colourful quilt, this time in creams and yellows. A photo of Chiara with her mother adorned the dresser, flanked by two scented candles waiting to be lit.

'How on earth did you get all this done so fast?'

Her flush deepened. 'It's just paint. You've been having to replaster walls and mess around with tiles.'

But it wasn't just paint. Each floor had been a painstaking job for a start. And it was all the touches: the paintings and photos, the new towels waiting in the wardrobes, matching robes on the back of the doors, that turned a simple redecoration into something more.

'I don't know what to say, how to thank you.'

'I enjoyed it. No thanks necessary.' Her voice turned brisk. 'So, I am planning to put a second coat of varnish on the spare room floor. Yours should have dried but be careful on it tonight, then I can get painting them tomorrow. Are you still happy with the sage green for your room and that light grey-blue for the spare room?'

'More than happy, but I forbid you to do another second's work today,' Joshua told her sternly. 'You are meant to be on vacation.'

'I told you, I like to keep busy…'

'You can busy yourself with a glass of wine while I cook you dinner.'

'No need, honestly.'

'Rebecca, this isn't a request, it's an order. You may not pick up another paintbrush until you've been suitably wined and dined. And while we eat, we need to talk about payment. It's been all renovation and no sightseeing for the last seven days.'

She protested again but allowed Joshua to shepherd her to the sofa and place a glass of wine in her hands while he started to chop some vegetables. They'd eaten together most evenings since Thanksgiving, but it had been quickly grabbed food after a busy day: pizza, salad, Chinese takeout from the excellent restaurant in Newington. A home-cooked meal was new. More intimate, with the uncorked wine, the fire roaring in the stove.

'You chop like a professional,' she said as he pushed the peppers to one side and grabbed the courgette. 'Chef, handyman, trail guide, is there no end to your skills?'

'I can't bake, not even with a packet mix, but working my way up in a hotel meant stints in every part, including the kitchen. I cleaned rooms, bussed tables, worked the desk, waited on guests, concierged... If my staff do it I have tried it. Some things more successfully than others, admittedly. My grandfather insisted my father learn the trade from the ground up before moving into a manager's office and my father did the same for me. And then I made it clear that Marco and Chiara were both expected to put some time in learning all the jobs that make a hotel successful too.'

'They've followed you into the hotel business?'

'Yes, Marco, as you know is our Managing Director. He's checking in on our recently launched Rome hotel at the moment, not that I have any worries. It's being run by Eleanora, who is one of the best hotel managers I have ever trained. Rome's gain is New York's loss there.'

'And Chiara?'

Joshua could feel his face pull into a worried frown and tried to summon a smile. 'She's in the hotel business too but doesn't work for us. She moves from job to job. She's not ambitious, Chiara, not like her brother. She's more interested in visiting as many countries as she can than a career.'

'Doesn't sound too bad to me.'

'No,' he conceded. 'She has certainly crammed a lot in so far. And I was absolutely supportive of her travelling. But it's a way of life now, not a gap year or two. Her mother always wanted to travel—she kept a list of places to visit when the kids were grown up and we could take our own gap year, but it wasn't to be. Chiara always wanted to live her mother's dreams. But where will it end? Will she ever settle down?'

It felt freeing to share his worries. He didn't like to sound less than supportive of his daughter, dwelling on where she was rather than what she was doing there—usually a badly paid entry level position. But he was worried by her lack of stability. Of course Chiara would always be able to get a job at any Grand York hotel she wanted, but by now he had hoped she would settle into a career.

'Where was top of Gabriella's list?' Rebecca's gaze was gently interested. 'If you don't mind me asking?'

'Not at all.' He pushed the courgette to one side, looking over at their wedding photo in pride of place on the wall. 'You know, the worst part when she died, apart from her actual absence, was the way no one wanted to talk about her. I guess they didn't know what to say so they said nothing at all. But I *wanted* to talk about her, to remind the world she was here and she was wonderful. It was raw then. But now, after all this time, I've learned to be thankful for what we did have rather than bitter about what we lost. So many people never really love, and I had over twenty years. I was a lucky man.'

'You were.' Her voice was quiet and Joshua mentally kicked himself. He'd forgotten that her love story had soured.

'Gabriella really wanted to visit South America. She loved colour and food and music. Brazil was at the top of her list.'

'And you?'

'Europe for me, especially Italy. Also for the food. And the history. And did I mention the food?'

'Let me guess, you like Italian food?'

'My mother and wife were both Italian, it's in the genes.'

'That must be it.' She paused. 'What was it like? Falling in love so young? Knowing you'd found your soulmate so young.'

Joshua checked the pan of boiling water and added some pasta to it before heating some oil ready for the herbs he'd chopped earlier

'I fell in love with Gabriella the first time I saw her. She'd only just moved to New York, to the States. She turned up at school and I took one look and fell hard. We all did.' He grinned. 'I was three.'

She laughed. 'Early starter.'

'It took a while to woo her. We lived in Brooklyn, in a big Italian neighbourhood. Man, we had some good times.' He laughed softly, thinking of his often idyllic childhood. 'I asked her out when we were fourteen, to Homecoming. She said yes. And that was it.'

'That is so romantic.'

'Not always.' He threw the vegetables into the oil, enjoying the sizzle. 'A teen pregnancy wasn't romantic. Telling our parents that we were having a baby and getting married straight after graduation definitely wasn't romantic. In the end they took it as well as could be expected and paid for an apartment while I studied, but otherwise made it clear it was down to us. I was at college, Gabriella trying to get some credits at night school. Then, after I finished college, it was her turn. She was studying to be a nurse and I was working in the hotel when Chiara came along. At times we were ships that passed just close enough to throw the kids to each other in a never-ending game of tag. Meanwhile, our friends were going out, having fun. At times it was really hard.'

'But you made it.'

'We did. She became a nurse, the kids were at school, my hours settled the more senior I got, we bought a house. We made time for each other.' He added the chopped tomatoes and anchovies. 'We grew up together.'

Rebecca took the plate Joshua held out and carried it over to the table, sniffing appreciatively. 'That smells so good.'

Deceptively simple, it was perfectly cooked, the pasta al dente, the vegetables sweetly charred, a subtle blend of herbs she couldn't quite identify brought out by the umami in the anchovies and cheese. More, it was a meal cooked for her with care and attention. She couldn't remember the last time that had happened.

They ate slowly, enjoying every forkful, every sip of wine, discussing the progress made on the cabin so far and their plans for tomorrow.

'Are we on track?' she asked. 'We're on the first December, so you have how long? Just over three weeks until your family arrives?'

'Thanks to you, we are way ahead of schedule. The bedrooms and bathrooms should be finished in a few days, then I can start down here.'

'The downstairs won't take half as long. The new furniture is due on the twenty-first and the kitchen worktop will be fitted the day before that.'

'You know, it's not just that you're a dab hand with a paintbrush and sander, you are also a great project manager,' Joshua said. 'I would probably have concentrated on one room at a time, but you have a conveyer belt of jobs going. Floors drying in one room, sanding in the other, varnishing frames in a third. I thought I could multi-task but you're on another level.'

Rebecca's cheeks heated. It wasn't that she was unused to compliments, but so many were about how she looked, her strength, her grace, her beauty. Even four years at the helm of her company hadn't quite dispelled that. Every interview or profile began with a rundown of her looks—her dancer's body, long legs and neck, the colour of her hair, shape of her eyes. She was repeatedly asked about what it was like as a woman at the top as an ex-dancer. And, of course, married to Ivan, articles had speculated on her childlessness, her decision to stay in New York and not join him in LA. No interview with Ivan dwelled on that decision in the same way. To be appreciated for her mind, even in such a small way, gave her a glow of pleasure that warmed her through.

'Everything is choreography,' she explained and laughed at the stunned look on his face. 'On stage you have to know where everything and everyone is and everything and everyone must have a purpose. As a new dancer you may literally be propping up a pillar in the market in *Romeo and Juliet*, but you can't just stand there; you have to be in character, be aware where everyone is. And then, when you come to direct yourself, you need to convey that. To juggle all those characters, steps, props, sets, lights, costume, hair and make-up so to the audience it's one seamless ballet. I need to know how long each costume change, hair change, set change is to the second. The choreography extends beyond the steps.'

'And if it goes wrong?'

'We have to try and hide it if we can. Dancers learn quickly to kick stray props out the way, to whirl into the wings to fix a ribbon, to modify a step or a jump and to keep in character the whole time. Hotels must be the same, surely?'

'Absolutely. I had a head chef quit on me during service one night: just walked out, leaving half the meals uncooked.'

'What did you do?'

'Promoted everyone up one rung on the spot and took over the washing-up. One of the diners said it was the best meal she'd had all stay.'

Rebecca put her fork down and picked up her wine. She loved how casually he'd mentioned that he'd pitched in with the most menial job. He was the CEO of a successful chain, an intelligent, handsome man, but he had no arrogance. It was part of what made him so very attractive.

'Was that the worst thing that has happened?'

He laughed. 'Not even close. And, no matter what it is, we have to sort it out. That's what people pay us for. Once a family left a child behind—they got two taxis and each thought the other had him. They were at the airport before they realised they were missing him. Meanwhile, my deputy was in a third taxi with the child and my receptionist was calling them like crazy. Another time we were holding a very fancy wedding when the celebrant got delayed. I had to get an online licence and step in. I had no idea what to say!'

'I bet you just smiled that charming grin of yours and everyone just fell into line.' As soon as the words were out she wanted to unsay them and she hurriedly added, 'But of course some people will complain, no matter what you do.'

'Sounds like you have experience of that yourself.'

'Oh, yes, you won't believe how many people ask for refunds! They were expecting singing, or couldn't follow the story, or we'd run out of their favourite wine and ruined the evening. It's crazy.'

'I bet they are the same people who finish all their food and then tell us it wasn't right and they want the bill waived.'

'Probably on the same evening!'

Joshua sat back, pushing his plate away. 'What's the funniest mishap that's happened to you on stage?'

'Funniest? They never seem that funny at the time.' She thought hard. 'Once a dancer managed to pirouette right into the orchestra pit. It could have been disastrous but luckily she was okay—as was the trombonist she landed on—and the trombone!'

He laughed, a slow appreciative rumble she felt right through her.

'Another time I was dancing this *pas de deux*…it was a very serious piece and our costumes were almost Grecian, wrapped round us, and my partner's just started to unravel while we danced.'

'What did you do?'

'What could we do? We danced on until he was practically bare-chested and then he just moved into the wings, where a dresser was waiting, and I improvised until he could join me! Another time, my wig fell off. I just kicked it into the wings and carried on, my hair in this very unflattering net!'

'I'm sure you looked beautiful.'

His voice was low, his gaze hypnotic, and Rebecca swallowed. 'I…' And then she caught sight of the view behind him. The outside lights were on and, clearly illuminated, were snowflakes dancing down past the window, at first just a few and then more and more, now falling quickly. 'Snow, oh, Joshua, snow!'

He blinked, as if slowly released from a spell, and turned to look. When he looked back at Rebecca his eyes were sparkling. 'Come on!'

She didn't need to ask where or why. Giggling like children, they rushed to the door, pulling on coats and boots as Joshua flung the door open and they tumbled onto the porch. The snow had only been falling for a short while, but it already covered the ground in a sparkling velvety layer. Rebecca stood on the edge of the porch and tilted her face, letting the icy flakes settle on her eyelashes and mouth.

'Snow in New York always feels like such a nuisance,' she said, keeping her voice hushed, not wanting to intrude into the magical scene in any way. 'It means audiences unable to travel, dancers slipping and injuring themselves, disruption. But this? This is magical. It's so beautiful.'

'Yes,' Joshua said. 'It is.'

But when she turned to smile at him, he wasn't looking at the scenery. He was looking at her.

Rebecca swallowed, her stomach twisting

with nerves, a little fear, but, drowning out the negativity, desire—and hope.

'Joshua,' she half whispered.

She couldn't have said who took the first step, or the second, but the next thing she knew she was gazing up at him, the strong jawline, his firm mouth, the laughter lines around warm brown eyes, and she knew she could trust Joshua Pearson. That she did trust him. And she also knew that for him to look at her like this—with the same mingle of hope and desire—was a rare privilege.

They stood, as if poised in the wings, for one breathless moment and then his mouth was on hers, sweet and undemanding. A leisurely introduction, a question as to whether they both wanted the same things. Rebecca gripped his shoulders, holding onto firm muscle to anchor herself.

Time slipped away as, slowly, tentatively and then with greater confidence, they learned each other, the kiss deepening bit by bit. Rebecca pressed closer, her hands now slipping down Joshua's back, exploring muscles still evident beneath his coat before she fastened at his nape, bringing him closer to her. He held her lightly, but she could feel the burn at her waist where his fingers splayed. The coats were both an unwanted barrier and a welcome buffer, ensuring they didn't speed past the point of no return.

She couldn't have said how long they stood there. She didn't feel the cold, was no longer aware of the thickening snow, all she knew was him. All she wanted was him in a way she hadn't wanted for longer than she cared to remember, desire hot and dangerous and irresistible flickering inside her, every nerve aflame, every inch of skin desperate for touch.

It had been so long since anyone had touched her.

With that realisation reality intruded and, despite every cell telling her not to stop, Rebecca broke away from the kiss and shakily took a step back, still holding his sleeve like an anchor. 'I should go.'

Joshua looked like a man in a daze but at her words his expression cleared. 'It's freezing out here. Why don't you warm up before you head back? I can make some hot chocolate.'

Hot chocolate? Had he just experienced something different to the toe-curling, all-encompassing passion that had just enveloped her? Her expression must have shown her confusion because he drew her in for a moment and it was all she could do not to put her head on his shoulder, press against him and pretend he was hers.

'I'm not going to pretend I wouldn't like to warm you up in other ways, but I don't want to rush this or you.' His mouth quirked into a half smile. 'Or me. This is all new to me as well. So let's have a hot chocolate and discuss our plans for tomorrow. I owe you a day out and I would really like it to be a date.'

Despite all the doubts that had come rushing back, Rebecca couldn't help but smile. 'A date?'

His gaze was serious as he looked down at her. 'I haven't dated since Gabriella died. I haven't wanted to, despite lots of well-meaning friends trying to set me up and Chiara installing apps on my phone in a not too subtle hint. But I like you, Rebecca, I like you a lot, and I would very much like to take you on a date. If you want to. And if not,' he carried on hurriedly before she had a chance to reply, 'then I very much hope that this hasn't ruined the friendship between us. Because I know we haven't known each other long but I feel that we are friends. Don't you?'

'Yes,' she said, not allowing herself to overthink. 'I think we are. And yes, I would love to go on a date with you. And yes to the hot chocolate, because I can't actually feel my toes. Yes to it all.'

He laughed then before dropping a kiss on the top of her head, such an unconsciously affectionate gesture it almost undid her. 'Come on, then,' he said. 'Hot chocolate it is.'

CHAPTER FIVE

'SKIING?' REBECCA LOOKED at the snow-covered slope looming ahead and took a step back. 'I don't know. Besides, aren't beginners meant to start on the nursery slopes?'

It had been snowing steadily since the evening of the day before but there was still a fairly light dusting at ground level, just a few centimetres deep. However, the mountain slopes had a deeper covering that boded well for the season ahead. And today's impromptu date.

Joshua laughed. 'This is the nursery slope.'

'Oh.' She bit her lip. 'Is there a pre-nursery slope? Something flatter?'

'Any flatter and the skis wouldn't go at all.' He gave her a quick glance, trying to assess how much of her reluctance was nerves and how much she really didn't want to do this. Gabriella had never dissembled; she'd said what she thought no matter what. Rebecca was clearly more diplomatic.

'Okay.' She turned to face him, radiating determination. 'But before we start you need to know something about me.'

'Fire away.'

'A dancer needs many qualities to succeed. A physical aptitude, obviously, and for ballet a certain body shape is still required by many companies, regardless of talent. But, just as important, maybe most important of all, are certain mental qualities. Perfectionism and a good degree of competitiveness are very useful, channelled properly.'

'Which means?' He didn't try and hide his grin. He'd already seen both qualities in Rebecca over the last ten days. She liked to finish her tasks before him, clearly taking pride in sauntering in to him to tell him she was finished. And every task was finished to the highest level, her critical eye assessing and reassessing, tweaking and snagging continually.

'Which means I am terrible at learning new things,' she admitted. 'If I don't get it quickly and I don't have an aptitude for it, I can be a little moody. I'm not a great loser, and I am most competitive against myself. I can set impossibly high standards.'

'Noted.'

'I know I should have grown out of it by now but…'

She looked adorably uncertain of herself, and Joshua couldn't resist pulling her in and dropping a kiss on top of her head, instantly transported back to last night and the kiss in the snow. He had felt like a teenager again, overwhelmed by the contact, the sensation, the way he had been completely lost in the moment, oblivious to the chill of the snow, the dark, to anything but the feel and taste of her.

He didn't know how he felt about it. On one hand exhilarated and full of anticipation for what the next few weeks would bring, on the other apprehensive. One thing he didn't feel was guilt, which was both unexpected and a relief. Instead he got the sense that Gabriella would be pleased he had finally taken a step forward. Would she have liked Rebecca? The two women were very different but they both had an innate honesty and shared the same determined spirit.

'We don't have to do this,' he reassured her. 'There are lots of quaint towns and some interesting historical buildings in Vermont; we could visit some of those if you prefer. It's not the maple season, sadly, but there is a cheese trail I've always wanted to try.'

'A cheese trail?'

'Lots of artisan cheesemakers. I am more than happy to spend the day appreciating cheese if you'd rather. I just knew you had never had the chance to learn to ski and thought you might like the chance to try, but no worries if not.'

She worried at her bottom lip as she looked around. 'That child can barely be old enough to walk.' She nodded at a small tot steadily skiing down the slope, a beaming smile directed at everyone it passed. 'I am going to be shown up by a child in diapers.'

'Does that mean you'll give it a go?'

'Yes.' She nodded, head high, looking more as if she were going to face lions rather than strap some skis to her feet. 'But no photographic evidence, please.'

'Not until you can do the perfect snowplough,' he promised. 'And as a reward…'

'Now you mention a reward?'

'When we drove up here, did you notice the resorts further down?'

'I did.'

'I've booked us in for an afternoon of après-ski spoiling. There are hot tubs and open-air swimming pools, steam rooms and massage rooms. The season has barely opened so they were happy to accommodate a last-minute booking.'

'Joshua Pearson, you know exactly how to incentivise a woman.'

'Come on, then, let's go hire you some skis.'

It didn't take long to sort Rebecca out with boots, skis and poles and Joshua taught her to slide along the level and to bend her knees as she went. As he had expected, she was a quick learner, her grace and balance aiding her as she, gingerly at first, made her way from the rental towards the slopes.

Joshua had offered to hire an instructor, but Rebecca took one look at the various cheerful youths coaxing small children into bending their knees and shook her head decisively. 'If you want to go and do some proper skiing then of course,' she said. 'But if you are willing and able I would much rather you show me.'

'And in return you can give the ballet class you have been promising me,' he said with a grin and her eyes narrowed as she looked him up and down.

'You're in good shape for a man in his fifties with a desk job, but ballet can strengthen muscles and ligaments, help with flexibility and provide core strength. I'd be happy to give you some pointers.'

'Any time. Right, first lesson, the ski lift.'

As befitted a nursery slope, the lift was a simple grab and be pulled affair, which soon got them to the halfway point where he planned to start her first lesson. She yelled in surprise when he told her to let go but managed to slide away from the lift without falling over.

'Learning to exit a ski lift is an art,' he said, steadying her. 'It feels counterintuitive to just push yourself off, but you did really well.'

She just nodded as she stared down the slope. It was an easy starter run, just twenty metres long and a gentle gradient, but her expression suggested she was staring down a black run of pure ice.

'The second lesson is how to stop.'

'I approve of this lesson!'

Joshua had suspected that Rebecca would have a natural aptitude and he was proved right. The first few goes he kept her slow and steady, snowploughing as much as skiing, concentrating on posture, knees and turning so she was descending the slope in a graceful zigzag. It wasn't all smooth sailing as she tumbled over more than once, but once she was reassured by the way her skis released and the easy landing, she took it in her stride, although she carefully tested her ankles and knees each time before starting again.

For the seventh try he took her to the top of the nursery run and, to his delight, she managed a smooth descent, whooping as she came to a stop at the bottom. Her cheeks were pink, her eyes bright and wisps of hair escaped her hat as she pulled him in for a triumphant hug.

'I did it! I skied!'

'You did brilliantly. I reckon we can get you on a green slope. Want to try it?'

There was no hesitation in her expression. 'Absolutely.'

'The chair lifts are a little different to the pull ones,' he warned her. 'There's a slim margin when you can easily ski off them so wait for my signal.'

Rebecca didn't just ski the green slope once. It was well into the afternoon by the time he called a halt. 'I know you are insanely fit, but you are probably using muscles you've not used before.' He wasn't entirely sure about the accuracy of the statement; ballet dancers probably used every muscle. 'And we can come back any time.'

Rebecca was glowing. It was the only word

for it, not just from the cold and exercise but from the achievement. 'Can we?'

'Absolutely. You only learned the real basics today. There's a lot more to learn.'

'I thought I'd hate it but I loved it. The speed was exhilarating.'

'It gets addictive,' he agreed.

She slanted him a knowing glance. 'Thank you. You must have been bored senseless. That slope felt like a real achievement to me, but you could probably ski it in your sleep. If we do come back, I am happy to get an instructor if you want to do something more challenging, or I could even practice by myself.'

'Not at all,' he protested. And he meant it. As a sport, the day had lacked challenge, true, but as an experience he wouldn't have missed a second. Watching Rebecca progress from doubtful beginner to this exhilarated enthusiast had been every bit as satisfying as a challenging run. More so, in fact, because the day had been filled with laughter and companionship.

'Well, next time I insist you spend at least an hour on a more difficult run. You could now. I can get a hot drink and wait for you.'

'That's a kind offer, and I will take you up on it next time, but right now we have the second half of our date to enjoy, so let's return your skis and head to it.'

He turned to look at the mountain as they headed towards the hire centre, watching a young couple on the ski lift, heads close together. His chest tightened as he watched them. They reminded him of weekends spent in this spot, the children in ski school and he and Gabi heading up the slopes for some child-free sport. He had found it hard to ski without her, to find the same pleasure in the pastime. Today was a gift. Another step to not just living but finding joy in life. Each step came with a tinge of guilt, but at the same time a certainty that it wasn't just time, it was also what Gabi would have wanted. What he needed.

Twenty minutes later they were back in Joshua's car as he drove down to the bottom of the mountain. The roads were well gritted, and his car fitted with winter tyres, but snow had started to fall again and so he took it carefully. The resorts were clustered at the bottom of the mountain and, covered in snow, had taken on a fairy-tale quality. It was already getting dark and most of the hotels had been decorated for Christmas, giving the whole area a festive air. Everywhere

Joshua looked there were trees covered in lights, lanterns lighting up paths and other festive decorations.

He pulled in at a gleaming glass and stone complex illuminated with tasteful silver and white lights.

'Okay, part two begins.'

Rebecca didn't move to get out of the car. Instead she turned to look at him, her expression unreadable. 'When did you plan all this?'

'Last night.' He had a moment of doubt. 'Too much? I wanted to take you skiing but it can be quite gruelling the first time, so I thought some pampering afterwards would mitigate that. After all, you're working pretty hard physically at the moment, with all the decorating.'

'Oh, I see. You just want to ensure there's no slacking when we get back to it tomorrow.'

'Only ulterior motives. Is it though? Too much?' It had seemed like such a good idea at the time, but now he could see how intimate an afternoon spa break was, especially for a first date. 'I told you it's a long time since I dated. If I've got it wrong, say.'

'You're hoping we can do the cheese trail after all?'

'You're a mind reader.'

She didn't answer for a long moment and

then leaned in and brushed his mouth with hers, sweet and soft. 'No. Not too much. Maybe if we hadn't already spent all week with each other it might have seemed a little over the top, but under the circumstances...' She paused. 'It's thoughtful. Really thoughtful. Thank you.'

'That's me,' he joked. But the truth was he wasn't thinking, he was operating on instinct. He had no idea what this thing with Rebecca was. Was it a fling, two lonely people brought together by circumstance, learning to let go together? Or was it something more? They lived in the same city after all. The New York dating scene was a shark tank, one no one ever escaped from unscathed, at least that was Joshua's excuse for not having gone near it over the last decade. But dating Rebecca? That would be different. He knew her, he got her, he liked her—and he thought she felt the same way. But for all that he was beginning to feel that he was possibly, maybe, ready to get back out there, she was so newly divorced the ink was barely dry. How ready was she for something more than a handful of holiday dates?

And how ready was he really? It was one thing to fall into something on holiday, but was he ready to introduce anyone to his children, his friends, his in-laws? That was not just a whole other step, it was a chasm he had no idea how to start to cross.

Besides, the last thing he wanted was to have a *Where is this going?* talk. This was the first date. They had shared one kiss. They were adults. He was overthinking it.

And so instinct it was. After all, it had steered him right so far.

Rebecca didn't usually do relaxed. She had regular massages, but they were a tool, part of her kit to keep her body fit and flexible. She swam because it was excellent exercise. She sat in steam rooms because heat was good for tired muscles—and ice for the same reason. But she didn't usually indulge in pamper sessions. Every second counted in her day. A spa trip had always felt like an indulgence too far.

Maybe she had been wrong.

No, she had *definitely* been wrong.

She kept her eyes closed as the beautician continued to rub something delicious-smelling into her face and the masseuse did something to her calves that just avoided pain but felt amazing nonetheless. Since arriving in the spa she had enjoyed a mud bath, followed after a much-needed shower by a seaweed wrap. The massage and facial were the end of the scheduled treatments, leaving her free to enjoy the heated outside pool and hot tub, the various steam rooms and sauna or, if she preferred, to wrap herself in the decadently soft gown and lie on one of the padded beds or hammocks.

It all sounded amazing.

Fifteen minutes later she tottered to one of the beds. Every muscle was relaxed and every inch of skin so soft she could take on a baby in a freshest skin competition. She sat down and contemplated the pool, knowing she'd regret not swimming but unsure how she'd get the motivation to get back up.

'Tea, madam?'

She nodded her acceptance to the smiling maid and took the fragrant jasmine tea and the accompanying tiny biscuits, more air than food. 'I want to move in,' she said aloud.

'Me too. Let's do it.'

She hadn't heard Joshua approach. He sat opposite and leaned over to take one of her biscuits. He wore just a pair of swim shorts and Rebecca felt the air whoosh from her body as she took him in.

Forget good for fifty, Joshua Pearson would be fine at any age. His body was lean with strong, defined muscles in all the right places. He'd clearly been swimming, his hair slicked back and drops glistening on his body, highlighting the definition. The desire she had been keeping at bay all day rushed back, weakening her knees and pooling in the pit of her stomach.

'How were your treatments?'

'Bliss. What about you?'

'I went for the Mountain Man treatment.'

She raised her eyebrows. 'Sounds testosterone-filled.'

'It's meant to be a way of making treatments appeal to the rugged outdoor types, but I agree, the branding needs work.'

'So, what's in the Mountain Man treatment?'

'A glacier facial, an insane massage that worked those kinks all out and something that involved hot clay.'

'Do you feel ready to tackle a mountain?'

'Actually, I feel ready for a good dinner and a snooze.'

She handed him the plate of biscuits. 'Here, these may help.'

Joshua regarded them dubiously. 'I prefer a little more substance in my snacks.'

Rebecca closed her eyes, soaking in the heat. The poolside was kept so warm, it was almost like being in the Caribbean rather than Vermont. Thanks to the earliness of the season and the fact it was a weekday, they had the place to themselves. Which made her all the more aware that Joshua was lying there almost naked, and she had on a bikini under her now too-hot robe. She could have selected a different bathing suit from the shop, a nice sturdy all-in-one that covered more than it revealed, but vanity had pushed her towards a flimsy green number.

'I need a swim,' she said, jumping to her feet and heading towards the pool. She kept the robe on until the last possible minute then let it slither off as she dived straight into the pool.

The water was warm, almost too warm, and so she set out to swim over to the glass panel that separated the outside from the inside, taking a quick breath and diving underwater before remerging in the outside pool. It was dark now, the pool area lit up subtly, the air cold and bracing, a sharp contrast to the warmth of the water. Rebecca breathed in, filling her lungs as she headed to the far end. The resort was lit up at one end of the pool, the other looked out onto darkness, lights here and there high in the mountains highlighting lodges and houses, the gondola lift and cars ascending and descending. But, despite all those signs of humanity, it was as if she were alone.

Almost alone.

She had known Joshua would follow her in, would interpret the flirtatious glance over her shoulder as she dived as an invitation and, sure enough, he surfaced beside her. Rebecca trod water, turning to face him, and before she could think of all the reasons that this was maybe a bad idea, that she should slow down and think things through, she kissed him, backing him up against the edge of the pool.

She felt as much as heard his rumble of surprise and amusement—and desire—and then he was kissing her back, sure and deep and with an intent that left her breathless. She could feel him tight against her, every muscle and sinew, and she pressed even harder, learning by feel what she had appreciated by sight. The kiss deepened, all-consuming as she forgot where she was. All she knew was Joshua, her hands gripping his shoulders, her legs entwined around his. Just like the evening before, seconds, minutes or hours could have passed before the sounds of voices passing by on the other side of the wall recalled her to herself and Rebecca propelled herself back, breathing hard.

'I...' But she had no idea how to finish the sentence.

She sneaked a look at him and was relieved to see that he seemed as dazed as she was. 'Damn, Rebecca,' he said, his voice hoarse. 'That was...' He shook his head.

'Good, bad, indifferent, inappropriate?'

'Incredible. And all I want to do is pull you close and do it again, but we were lucky not to have an audience that time.'

Rebecca swam next to him and anchored herself to the side of the swimming pool, thinking fast. She'd never been impulsive where romance was concerned, her love life a faraway second to her career. Even her marriage had been driven more by Ivan's determination. He'd swept her off her feet, true, but she'd not done the same back, allowing him to come to her, to make all the running. Looking back, that should have been a sign. But in every other part of her life she reached out for what she wanted, worked for it, took it.

She was a free woman and Joshua Pearson made her feel desirable. He made her feel alive. More than that, he made her laugh and seemed to respect her for attributes beyond her success and her looks.

And she wanted him. Maybe more than she had ever wanted any man before.

It terrified her and exhilarated her. Ivan had told her she was dead inside and she had believed him. Had wondered if something was missing, if her need to put her career before her marriage meant she was lacking in some way.

She might have just done her best to seduce Joshua Pearson in a swimming pool but surely it proved that she was flesh and blood.

Definitely blood. She could feel it coursing around her veins, her pulse going at twice its normal speed.

'Part of me wants to suggest we get a room here,' she said, and his eyes darkened. 'And part of me wants to run and hide,' she continued.

'Rebecca…'

'But I am enjoying getting to know you. I know we're grown adults, with lived lives and experiences, and no one would judge us for jumping into a thing here, but could we take it slowly?' She was shivering as she spoke, not from cold but desire, and mostly from nerves, for being so honest. For exposing herself so emotionally.

'Hey, Rebecca.' Joshua tilted her chin up

so she had no choice but to look into his open gaze. 'I get it. I feel the same.'

'You do?'

He nodded. 'I would like nothing more than to get a room and for us to finish what we just started and then do it all again. And there is part of me that just wants to head back to New York and pretend this didn't happen, not because of you—because you are pretty damn amazing—but because of what feeling like this means for me. It's a huge change. A change that has been a long time coming, and one I didn't realise I was anywhere near ready for. It's a lot.' He laughed softly. 'I'm probably making no sense.'

'You are. You are making total sense.'

'So taking it slow, getting to know each other more, dating, that sounds like something we would both be comfortable with. So maybe that's something we should do. Why don't we go and get dressed and I'll treat you to dinner here then drive you home like the perfect gentleman I am trying hard to be?'

'I'd like that, but I have one condition.'

'Name it.'

She smiled up at him. 'Dinner's on me. It's my turn,' she added as he began to protest. 'You cooked last night and organised this amazing day. It's the least I can do.' Her heart began to pound as he looked at her seriously.

'Okay then, it's a deal.'

Relief flooded her as he bent his head and kissed her briefly but sweetly. Ivan had had so much more money than her that he had been amused when she'd offered to pay, brushing her aside as if her job and the excellent salary it gave her was of no concern. It might seem a small thing, but Joshua's lack of macho pride and respect for her request was as sexy as his six-pack and broad shoulders.

She sighed internally as Joshua pulled away and began to make his way back to the inside pool, watching his strong, powerful body as he cut through the water. Taking things slowly was her idea and she knew it was the right thing to do—but she'd be taking a long cold shower before dinner. And, judging by the way her body was reacting, every day from now until Christmas.

CHAPTER SIX

'OKAY, ARE YOU READY? It's pretty dusty,' Joshua warned Rebecca as he lowered the box.

'As long as there are no dead mice or birds,' she said, arms up to receive it. 'Or spiders.'

'Just how dirty do you think my attic is?' he asked mock indignantly and she laughed.

'It's three years since you were last up there and you had roof tiles missing. An entire woodland family could have moved in.'

Joshua swept his torch around. Luckily the missing tiles had been on the outer parts of the roof and the attic had stayed dry. Rebecca was right, it was pretty filthy though and with more cobwebs than he suspected she would be comfortable with. He made a note to come up here with a damp cloth and broom and to have a sort-out before he left. There were things in here older than Chiara!

He stacked the other two boxes of Christmas

decorations by the loft hatch and then carefully lowered them to Rebecca one at a time.

It was incredible how much progress they had made on the cabin. Another week of hard work meant that, two weeks into December, the bulk of the work was done—and they'd even found time to head back to the ski slopes several times before or after work. The two upstairs bathrooms were retiled, and new taps and towel rails installed before both rooms had been repainted, and all the bedrooms were now finished. The downstairs floor had been varnished and the kitchen cabinets painted a soft sage green with new handles fitted. All Joshua was waiting for was the new sofas and chairs he'd ordered to replace the old and for the fitter to come and install the new worktops, both of which would happen next week, a few days before Marco and Chiara were due.

What made the whole thing perfect was that the cabin hadn't been suddenly transformed into a luxury home; it was still the same homely vacation house he and Gabriella had painstakingly restored, it had just been updated and given a new lease of life. Rebecca had understood that and stuck to the brief, even carefully reframing some of the better family pictures, including his wedding photo. Despite the fact they seemed to be getting closer every day, she displayed no signs of insecurity about Gabriella and their marriage; rather she seemed to intuitively know what to say, what to ask, how to react when he talked about his wife and his marriage.

And now here they were, about to sort through the Christmas decorations. Every year decorating the tree had been difficult, with so many memories attached to every bauble and ornament. Despite the three-year gap, Joshua expected this year to be no exception. But just as the cabin was the same but better, so would Christmas be, and he planned to keep out only the best decorations and buy some new. The old ones would be returned to the attic as he wasn't ready to actually discard anything for good—and, after all, the children might want them. Not that Chiara had a home of her own and Marco didn't really go in for decorating his apartment, but one day...

'Okay, boss, what's the plan?' Rebecca asked as Joshua placed the last of the three boxes on the sitting room floor. 'Are you going to get the tree today?'

He shook his head. 'Not until Marco and Chiara get here—we'll choose one in the forest on Christmas Eve.'

'I sense a tradition.'

'One of my favourites. Christmas starts early at the hotel; we actually start decorating during Thanksgiving. It takes a lot of time and careful planning. There are several trees, including the famous eighty-footer on the roof, and they all need to wow our guests.'

'I love that tree; it's as much a sign Christmas has arrived as the Rockefeller tree.'

'You're not the only one and we know that we have a reputation to uphold so we take Christmas very seriously. Every weekend is full of activities, most traditions repeated year after year and our guests wouldn't have it any other way.' He opened one of the boxes and more dust swirled into the air. Rebecca jumped up and headed to the kitchen, returning with a couple of cloths. He took one gratefully.

'You get a lot of repeat bookings at this time of year then?' she asked as she sat next to him. Her faint floral scent enveloped him. 'I hope you recommend a trip to the ballet.'

'I will from now on,' he promised. 'And yes. We get repeat guests all year round but especially at Christmas. Because I had a young family, and because I grew up around the hotel myself and, as Gabi often worked nights or weekends, the children spent a lot of time at work with me and so they got used to celebrating every holiday with guests. As I said, Christmas begins early with the decorating of the hotel and then we put on a whole host of family-friendly Christmas activities, from gingerbread house building to carol concerts. As time went on, we've added more to the programme and our seasonal celebrations have become famous. Families come to New York at Christmas year after year just to stay with us; in fact, guests who first came as children now bring their children to experience the magic.'

'That's wonderful.'

'It is.' This was the first year he had missed it—and with Marco in Rome the first year no Pearson was personally hosting Christmas at the Grand York. He thought he might miss the familiar sounds and smells and people, but he was more than content up here. Very content, in fact, which was something he needed to think through.

'It is,' Joshua repeated. 'But it's also a lot. So we would drive up here Christmas Eve to spend Christmas just us. Chop the tree and decorate it, then in the evening we would watch Christmas movies with milk and cookies until the children finally fell asleep.'

'And that's what you're planning to do this year?'

'Every single second,' he said.

Over the years certain parts of the tradition had slipped away. He didn't often get both kids for a start, and it was a while since they'd all settled down with milk and cookies, but this year he wanted to celebrate them all being together by recreating it all.

'I know you are on top of stockings,' Rebecca said. 'But have you thought about new Christmas pyjamas?'

'Matching ones?'

'Up to you.'

'It's a good idea; I'll add it to the list. There's a Christmas market this weekend. I'm planning to get the rest of the presents there.'

He had been collecting presents for the kids' stockings for a few weeks. Nothing big: some local maple toffee, Christmas socks, chocolate coins, a newly framed photograph from the collection on the wall. Luckily, he'd brought their main presents with him, as if he'd had a presentiment that he was going to end up staying in Vermont until they arrived. He'd had his grandfather's watch cleaned and mended for Marco and Gabriella's engagement ring cleaned for Chiara, commissioning matching earrings. It was a modest diamond and amethyst ring befitting their youth and circumstances, but Gabriella had loved it, refusing to allow him to replace it when he'd offered for their twentieth anniversary.

'Okay, so no tree until Christmas Eve. Are you going to do any earlier decorating at all?'

'I'll get a wreath from the market, some holly and mistletoe. And put some of these ornaments out now. I want it to feel Christmassy when they arrive.'

'Hot chocolate simmering on the stove, gingerbread cookies in the oven...'

'Do you think I'm a nostalgic old fool?'

'I think you are a wonderful father and that they are very, very lucky to have you.' Her eyes were wistful and Joshua wondered if she were thinking about the parents who had never taken an interest in her life or the husband who brought pain to her voice no matter how bright her smile.

'Okay, let's take a look at these boxes,' he said, pulling out the first ornament, carefully wrapped in tissue. 'Shall we make three piles? One for anything we can use to decorate now, one for things to put back in the attic and one for the decorations for the tree.'

'Aye, aye, Captain.'

* * *

Rebecca was fascinated as Joshua started to sort through the boxes: fascinated and yet a little uncomfortable. Partly because this was so personal a business. Yes, they had progressed to a real friendship spiced up by the acknowledged attraction and yes, they seemed to be able to open up to each other, but being part of this activity was a step beyond an intimate conversation. This was allowing her to see right into the heart of his family, a privilege she wasn't sure she was ready for.

And partly because it was yet another reminder of how families could be. She'd always laughed off the Christmas movie vision of family traditions as an advertiser's version of what Christmas should be, not the reality. After all, her family's Christmas had depended on what pageants were happening where and on more than one occasion had been celebrated in motels on the way to or from a competition or even split, Rebecca and her dad at home, her mother and sisters on the road. Then, when she was older, Christmas was about work and it was such a busy time, decorating was very much an afterthought. Ivan had employed a professional company to do his house, Trudie and Anita the same.

Rebecca usually stuck up a wreath and a pre-lit twig tree and thought no more about it. After all, the theatre had all the decorations she could want.

But here were three boxes that represented much-loved traditions—and love. Joshua had had the perfect marriage, the perfect family. What was he doing with her?

She pushed the negative thoughts away determinedly and took the various baubles and decorations Joshua handed to her, wiping each one carefully before placing it on the allotted pile. It was clear straight away not much was heading back to the attic. Every one seemed to have a story or a sentimental attachment to it, and Joshua grew misty-eyed long before they had finished the first box.

'Gabi loved to travel,' he said, picking out a blue orb with a seascape on. 'And everywhere we went she bought an ornament for the tree. This is Cape Cod, where we spent our honeymoon. Three nights in a rundown motel on the outskirts of Provincetown. She said we'd have a real honeymoon one day, when the kids grew up, then we'd travel all round the world. But in the end she barely got to leave the States, beyond a week here or there when we could find the time.'

'Have you travelled much since Chiara left

home?' She took the bauble carefully, aware how much history was invested in its fragile glass shell.

'I've gone to visit Chiara a couple of times, scoped out possible venues for our expansion into Europe, checked out the competition, of course, but otherwise no.' He sat back, rubbing a hand across his forehead. 'Partly because travel was Gabi's dream and I didn't know where to start without her, or even if I wanted to. Partly because I felt I needed to be a stable point that the kids could rely on. And partly because work is how I got through my loss. I needed the routine, the stimulus, the absorption, and the great thing about hotels is that there is always something to do, whether it's three p.m. or three a.m. Travel would leave me too much time to think.'

'Work is how I manage my emotions too,' Rebecca said.

'Do you miss it?' His glance was keen.

'I needed a break,' she admitted, as much to herself as to him. 'I see that now. And I have loved helping you here. I got a real sense of achievement at the end of every task, every day...'

'But...'

'But I miss the studio,' she confessed. 'I miss being in class, watching rehearsals. I miss the moment the curtain opens, whether I'm backstage or front of house. I miss coaching and the moment I tell a dancer they are going to learn a new role. I even miss the budget meetings and the wooing of donors.'

'That's how I feel about the hotels,' Joshua said unexpectedly. 'I like being there at four when check-in opens and people walk into the lobby for the first or thirtieth time and doubletake when they see the grand staircase and whatever seasonal theme we have going on. I love every bit, walking the dining rooms to see if the tables are laid correctly, checking out the rooms are properly prepared or ensuring an event is going well, and I love the business side, whether that's planning for the next season or looking at expansions. Lately I seem to have lost that buzz. Maybe by letting Marco spread his wings I have clipped mine.'

'So what are you going to do?' If Rebecca knew anything about the man opposite it was that he wasn't the type to sit back and feel sorry for himself.

The gleam in his eyes confirmed her suspicions. 'I have thoughts… They're not clear yet, but they're there.'

Rebecca laughed. 'Mysterious!'

'That's me. Tall, dark and mysterious.' He put the box he'd been unpacking aside and opened the second box, unwrapping the first ornament. His face softened. 'Chiara's first Christmas.' He handed her the red and green bauble. 'We got it made specially. There's a matching one for Marco and another we had decorated for me and Gabi, celebrating our first Christmas together.'

'I am so sorry,' Rebecca said impulsively. 'She sounds like a wonderful person...you must miss her very much.'

He didn't answer at first. Instead Joshua stood up and strode over to the fridge, grabbing two bottles of beer and bringing them back over to the table, handing one to Rebecca. He took a long gulp before sitting back down and taking out the next two baubles, the one for Marco and the one commemorating his marriage. He turned the red orb over and over in his hands, his expression faraway.

'Gabi was so full of life,' he said at last. 'When she got the diagnosis we were shocked, of course, worried, but at the same time we completely believed she would beat it. She was barely forty, healthy, she ate well, didn't drink too much, exercised, she had a really good chance, the doctor told us. But of course the cancer didn't listen to the doctor. When we realised it was terminal...' He took another long gulp. 'I never want to live through another day like that again.'

'I can't imagine,' Rebecca said softly.

'Telling Marco, telling Chiara…' He shook his head. 'I'll never forget the scream Chiara gave. It was torn from her. Sometimes I still hear it in my nightmares. But Gabi was determined to live every last moment to the full, and in a funny way some of my most cherished memories are of those last few months. Being here, a few days in Hawaii, a trip to the ballet.' He nodded at her. 'I think you were dancing. In fact you were, because I remember Gabi saying she was so happy she got to see you as Juliet.'

'I'm glad I helped, even if I didn't realise.'

'You must be part of so many people's precious memories, just like the hotel is.'

'It's not something I think about too much, but I do get letters and cards, even now, from people telling me how coming to watch me helped them through a hard time. But good art should transport people, whether it's a temporary emotion or something more profound. Ballet isn't just art, it's entertainment as well. It's easy to forget that, but if the audience aren't entertained then what is it for?'

'Exactly the same as the hotels. We offer a five-star luxury experience, but guests have to feel at home there, like their children are welcome, that they are welcome. I hate those hotels where you feel like you have to whisper and that if your shoes didn't cost a thousand dollars you don't fit in.'

It was nice to have found someone who got her, who had similar ideals, a similar work ethic. It had been a long time since she had made new friends; it would be good if she and Joshua could stay in touch. Which was why, intriguing as the attraction was, it was important to keep it in perspective. She didn't want hormones to ruin this friendship.

'The worst part,' he said after a while, still staring at the bauble. 'The worst part was how angry I sometimes felt. That Gabi got sick, that she didn't beat it, that we didn't get to have the time alone we had promised ourselves, that she didn't live her dreams, that I was powerless to help her.'

'Do you still feel that way?' she half whispered, knowing he was talking to himself as much as her.

'No,' he said with a deep sigh, one that seemed to come from his soul. 'I thought I did, I don't know when it faded, but no. Now I can look back and marvel at what we managed. Two kids who, against the odds, had over twenty years together, who raised two wonderful kids of our own, renovated this place, made a home, held down careers. It wasn't easy, there were times when the kids were small and one of us was always at work and we were exhausted all the time when we bickered a lot, but mostly we managed to love and to laugh. Some people never get that. I was lucky. We were lucky.'

'You were.' Rebecca hoped she managed to keep the longing and regret out of her voice. She and Ivan had had passion at one point, lived a luxurious life, but there had been very little laughter. How had she reached the age of forty-eight without realising how important laughter was?

'I will always miss her. Doing things we did together will always give me a moment's pause, a tinge of guilt, of pain, of loss. But happiness too. It's been a long journey to get to this point. I think renovating the cabin was the last thing I needed to do.'

Over the next half-hour they continued to sort through the boxes, putting the decorations for the tree in a crate in the much tidier coat cupboard so they could be easily accessed on Christmas Eve and the small handful Joshua had reluctantly decided he didn't need any more returned to the attic. Rebecca was charmed by his unashamed sentimental streak and his ease in sharing the stories evoked by the decorations. While a chicken roasted in the oven, they put up the decorations Joshua deemed okay to go up early: candles, silver and gold strings of lights, a nativity scene and other ornaments, including a family of deer Rebecca rather coveted.

It was easy to imagine the scene in a little under two weeks, Joshua welcoming his children into the cabin that had been the backdrop for so many happy memories. There would be hugs, maybe tears. The lights Joshua had entwined across the shelves and along the beams glowing, Christmas music playing, hot chocolate simmering on the stove, cinnamon cookies and gingerbread warming in the oven. Joshua had every detail planned. He wanted this to be a Christmas to remember.

And, after spending nearly every waking minute with him over the last few weeks, Rebecca would have returned to her own life.

It wasn't that she wouldn't be having a nice time. Anita and Trudie were also due on the twenty-third and were sending a decorator to install their tree and turn the cabin into a stylish Christmas paradise. They had reserved a table at the inn for dinner that evening and were hosting their famous Christmas drinks on Christmas Eve. Joshua might even call in—before the movies and hot milk part of his family traditions. It would be strange, being with him when he was surrounded by his children and she by her friends. This little idyll out of time would be over. And then she would be heading back, to her company, her theatre, her dancers.

She *wanted* to head back. She was relaxed physically, mentally and emotionally in a way she hadn't thought possible when she'd wearily put the cabin's coordinates into her hire car satnav. But she'd also been happy here, very happy. And that was down to Joshua, to their friendship, to the way he validated her. She could be herself with him in a way she had never been able to be with Ivan. Joshua actually seemed to like the real Rebecca. Liked her work ethic, liked her make-up-free in yoga pants, hair scraped back, liked her competitive independent spirit. He thought of ways to make her happy, rather than be angry that she wasn't happy fitting into his world.

But their time together wasn't at an end just yet. In just a couple of days they had planned a visit to the town's famous Christmas market, where she had been promised maple spiced cider and a sleigh ride in the snow.

There were also more ski trips over the next ten days—and there were bound to be more kisses. Sweet, soul-deep, toe-curling kisses with no expectation of more, just an acceptance of being completely in the moment. It wasn't that Rebecca didn't want more; she did. But there was a joy in stepping back to a world where dating meant kisses and hand holding and activities. It had been a decade since she had been with anyone but Ivan and she suspected that Joshua had only ever been with Gabriella. It suited them both to take things slow.

And of course there was laughter. Lots of it. Even when—especially when—things went wrong. It wasn't easy for a perfectionist such as herself to find the humour in a mistake, but Joshua's laid-back easy amusement changed that. Knocking over a tin of paint, ordering the wrong-sized sheet, missing a corner of the sanding—nothing fazed him; anything could and would be put right. She could see why he was such a good CEO—he was generous with praise, encouraging when teaching new skills, listened to ideas but had a clear vision, inspired you to want to be part of that vision. He had the perfect temperament for making guests feel at home and encouraging staff to be the best they could be.

She understood that, and wasn't that what she hoped to achieve herself? For her dancers to be inspired and her audience transported?

So why worry about tomorrow and how she might or might not feel? The here and now was good, more than good. Dinner was waiting, a fire crackled in the stove and a handsome, kind, interesting man was pouring wine.

Tomorrow and what came with it could most definitely wait.

CHAPTER SEVEN

'ARE YOU SURE this is safe?'

Joshua skated a little further out onto the lake and turned to face Rebecca, still on the shoreline, one foot gingerly testing the ice. 'Absolutely solid. I got word today. It's probably been safe for several days now, but the Perezes on the other side of the lake did a test earlier. Come on, I promise it won't crack no matter how often you fall.'

'Now, skating I can do,' Rebecca informed him. 'I'm just used to skating on a rink.'

'On a rink? Music and hot dogs and lights. This is *real* skating.'

'I've read *Little Women*. I know the dangers.' But she was now standing on the ice and taking a tentative step forward, testing the strength as she did so. Joshua liked that about Rebecca. She didn't rush in, didn't take someone else's word as gospel, she liked to know for herself. It showed an independence of thought and spirit he applauded.

'Okay,' she said, more to herself than to him, and sped up a little and then a little more until she had skated right past him, turning on an elegant edge to circle back round. 'Okay, I've got this.'

She was always graceful but here on the ice it was easy to see the dancer in her. The way she moved, the arc of her arms, the effortless-looking turns; although her thick jacket and hat and gloves were no tutu, her lines were still visible. Watching her gain confidence as she twirled and spun, Joshua's blood began to heat.

He wanted her.

It was no surprise; he'd admired her the day he'd first seen her, poised and contained, waiting by her car, and been struck by how attractive she was the next day when she'd come by to thank him. But it wasn't just her looks, although he loved running his hands through the silky strands of blonde hair and seeing the flecks of green and gold in her hazel eyes, admiring the long lean muscles honed by years of work, made more beautiful by their functionality.

She was an interesting companion, thoughtful and informed, easy to open up to. More than easy. Joshua hadn't been so candid with anyone in years.

But in many ways she was still a closed book. She volunteered little about herself, had skirted around the details of her divorce, but then it was all still so recent. He respected her desire for privacy, just as he respected her opinions and her determination to have a go, whether it was progressing to a harder ski slope or learning to tile.

He liked her, he respected her, he wanted her. Wanted to progress their physical relationship, to be with a woman who wasn't Gabriella. It was a lot to process. He'd never even really dated, as Gabi and he had fallen in love so innocently and quickly. And soon his children would be here. How would they feel if he was with another woman?

Which was why Rebecca's wish to take things slowly was more than okay. He was figuring all this out too.

'Are you going to skate or stand there daydreaming?' Rebecca called, wakening Joshua from his reverie, and he set off, skating towards her, faster and faster, grabbing her hand as she laughingly protested and pulling her alongside him as he raced around the curve of the lake, waltzing her round and round.

It was mid-afternoon but the winter sun had already sunk low, the snow-laden branches starting to silhouette against the purpling sky. Only a few cabins were occupied, their lights beacons dotted around the lake, otherwise they were alone in the world, in this frozen wonderland, as Joshua spun her to a stop, claiming her laughing mouth with a fierce possessiveness unlike any of the sweet, slow kisses they usually shared.

Rebecca grabbed his lapels to pull him in closer, kissing him back equally hard, taking as she gave. Time seemed to slow, as it always did when he was with her, lost in her, until the sound of distant voices could be heard as neighbours raced onto the ice, the children shrieking with laughter, telling them they were no longer alone.

Her eyes were huge as Rebecca pulled back, glazed, pupils dilated. She touched his cheek with one gloved hand, her slightly swollen mouth curving into a smile. 'Thank you.'

'The pleasure was all mine.'

Her smile widened. 'For the skates not the kiss. That was more of a joint endeavour.'

'Was it? I'd need to try it again to make sure…' He leaned in but she skated a few feet away, laughing.

'We have a Christmas fair to attend. I was promised cider and a sleigh ride.'

'I could make cider, light a fire…' he offered, but she shook her head.

'Decorating in return for seeing Vermont, remember? Besides,' she threw over her shoulder as she skated away, 'don't you have extra stocking presents to buy?'

Joshua admitted defeat as he skated after her. He had promised to take Rebecca out and about and had been looking forward to the small-town charm of the Christmas fair. And he did have more stocking presents to buy, plus some extras in case of unexpected guests. It wouldn't be unlike Chiara to rock up with a friend or two and, if so, they would also need stockings and a gift under the tree.

Plus it would be nice to get something for Rebecca. A memento of their time together.

But snuggling by the fire and continuing that kiss would have been nicer by far. Maybe later. They had planned a romantic sleigh ride after all…

'This is delightful!' Rebecca was doing her best to take in every sight and sound. She hadn't been to a small-town Christmas market since, well, she had never been to one and she was loving every second. The town choir were singing carols at the bandstand, smart in their matching striped hats and scarves, replacing a choir from the local school that had just finished their performance. Stalls featuring all kinds of local crafts lined the town square, selling everything from exquisite knitwear to gorgeous ceramics.

'So, what do you want to do first? Ferris wheel? Spiced hot cider? The sleigh ride?' Joshua held her hand freely. It was new, this easy public gesture of affection, but it fit. Fit the occasion, fit her mood.

Fit the promise hanging in the air. There had been a lot of kisses over the last couple of weeks, brief kisses, sweet kisses, long kisses, hot kisses, but nothing, not even the moment when she had practically jumped him at the spa, as deep, as carnal, as intense as the kiss on the ice—she couldn't believe they hadn't melted the ice beneath their skates.

'I'll meet you at the cider stall in an hour,' she suggested. 'I have some shopping to do.'

'As do I.' He pulled her in for a lingering kiss and she leaned in, enjoying how easy it all was. No pretending, no faking, just enjoying what they had.

Rebecca hadn't had an opportunity to do her Christmas shopping and took full advantage of the occasion, buying Trudie a pair of silver hoop earrings and Anita an orange cashmere scarf. Enchanted by a stall selling locally made candles, she ordered a couple of hampers full of them to be sent back to New York as gifts for her dancers and other staff. She also picked out a blue jumper for Joshua. She wasn't sure if they were doing presents, but it was perfect for winter walks. And he would look very sexy in it.

After less than a month she was turning into the kind of woman who lusted after men in knitwear. Maybe she had been doing the small-town thing too long after all.

She stopped by the stalls selling children's games and toys and wondered what her nieces and nephews liked. She saw them so seldom it was hard to get an idea of their interests. She sent gift cards at Christmas and for birthdays, chocolate at Easter and Valentine's, candy at Halloween, but they were impersonal gifts. Watching Joshua planning treats and surprises for his adult kids, hearing stories of Christmas traditions, she'd been aware of an ache of nostalgia. Not for a childhood she missed, but for the childhood and family she'd never had and hadn't created as an adult.

Her gaze drifted over to a small child whirling around, toes pointed, and she smiled. She didn't need to dwell on what she didn't have when she had so much. Her Christmas *did* include traditions. The Christmas Eve performance of *The Nutcracker* was always followed by gift-giving and the end of the run with a belated festive party using the set as a backdrop. She had friends she'd grown up alongside who she loved like sisters and who were always there supporting her when she needed it. And in many ways the company was her family; once she'd been the youngest and now she was the matriarch, and through all those years it had been the centre of her world.

And, much as she was enjoying *this* world, she was brimming with ideas for her return, itching to get back into class and full of anticipation for her return to the Academy. One of her favourite things was teaching the young dancers, with all of their enthusiasm and hope and potential, mentoring them as they grew.

'You look thoughtful.'

She hadn't seen Joshua and smiled up at him.

'Look at the children,' she said, nodding towards the grotto, where a line of excited small people were waiting to meet Santa. 'They're so excited.'

'I miss those days,' Joshua said as a small boy came leaping out, clutching a present to his chest, a beaming grin splitting his face almost in two. 'The unbearable anticipation, the excitement, the traditions, the utter belief in magic. Of course there was the time Chiara decided on Christmas Eve that she really wanted this particular pirate ship—I was that clichéd dad running from closing store to store while Gabriella was loading up the car to come here, time ticking away.'

'Did you find it?'

His smile was smug. 'Absolutely.'

'Of course you did. Your kids are so lucky; you are a great dad.'

'I don't know about great, but I do try my best.'

'That's all anyone could ask.' Was that what her parents would say? That they'd done their best? They might not understand her career, but they had allowed her to spend her childhood in the studio. They might not have supported her, but nor had they hindered her.

Maybe, after Christmas, she should pay them a visit. Take presents in person rather than sending the usual impersonal generic gifts.

She smiled at a small girl as she walked past, hugging a teddy to her chest. 'It must be lovely having little ones at this time of year.'

'You never wanted kids?'

It was such an innocuous question, an obvious lead from the opening she had left, and yet it caught her by surprise and all she could do was stammer incoherently. 'It's not that... obviously, I... I mean...'

'I'm sorry, I didn't mean to pry.'

'No, you're not. It's a reasonable question. It's just a bit complicated.'

'Then we can talk about something else. Or, even better, do something else. The line for the sleigh rides has died down and I believe that was top of our itinerary. Come on, we can grab some food when we get back.'

Rebecca should have been relieved that Joshua was so understanding—she *was* relieved—but at the same time she knew her reticence to discuss her divorce and all the implications with Joshua was because she was reluctant to confront her own feelings, the things Ivan had said, any culpability she had in the failure of her marriage. It wasn't like her to be such a coward, but the last year had left her so raw, she shuddered away from excavating the past. But she also knew that she would never move on until she did. Joshua had opened up to her. She knew he would listen, hoped he wouldn't judge—at least not as harshly as she judged herself.

They didn't have to queue for long and soon Joshua was handing her into the sleigh before swinging up to join her, putting an arm around her as the driver urged the horse to walk on.

'Having fun?' he asked, and Rebecca nodded. It wasn't exactly a lie. No one could help enjoying the perfect romantic scene with the sleigh ride; it was every bit the winter wonderland she'd been promised. A handsome bay horse pulled a sleigh straight out of a Victorian Christmas scene and she and Joshua were snuggled under a faux fur blanket as the horse pulled them along the snowy path along the river. It was a gorgeous winter's night, stars bright in a velvety dark sky, the moon a subtle glowing curve, and she snuggled against the broad shoulders that always made her stomach swoop and her pulse speed up and tried to be here in the now. She was with an attractive man who seemed to find her attractive, it was Christmas, snow covered the path and tree branches, and the only noise was the clip-clop of the horse's hooves and the jingling of his bridle. Even the driver added to the atmosphere with his peaked cap and cape.

It was just that, try as she might, she couldn't stop thinking about her family, her marriage, the steps she had taken that had led her here: forty-eight and divorced. She was a woman who set herself high standards, who hated to fail, and yet where these most important relationships in her life were concerned, she *had* failed. She hadn't even considered going to see her parents when her marriage ended and she needed to escape, had barely spoken to her sisters, and as for Ivan? A marriage ending was one thing, but to end in such bitterness and rancour was quite another.

'Yes,' she said, hoping that by saying it out loud she would completely mean it. 'Of course I am. This is gorgeous. Thank you for suggesting it.'

His arm tightened. 'So why don't I believe you?'

'I...'

'I shouldn't have asked you about children. It is completely none of my business.'

'It's not a big deal, honestly. It's just...' She turned to look at the frozen river, the trees silhouetted against the moonlit sky. 'Children are a huge part of the reason Ivan and I broke up, the reason it was so acrimonious. I thought that now the divorce was through I wouldn't dwell on any of it, that it was in the past, but I guess I haven't worked through it all as much as I thought.'

She knew she hadn't worked any of it through at all. That she had thrown herself into work and hoped all the pain would just go away.

'Do you want to talk about it? I'm a good listener.'

'No.' But that wasn't quite true. She did want to talk it through, and she wanted to talk it through with Joshua, but not right now. Not in this sleigh, not with the lights twinkling around them, not with the horse's breath clouding the air and the driver straight-backed in front of them. 'Not now. Let's enjoy the moment.'

'Of course, but any time, Rebecca, any time. I hope you know that.'

'I do.' She cupped his cheek, turning his face to hers so she could press a kiss onto his stubbled cheek. 'I absolutely do.'

They didn't speak for the rest of the sleigh ride, and by the time they pulled back up at the wait stop where the queue had once again lengthened, Rebecca had managed to restore her mood, eager to sample some of the delicious food and try the famous cider. Joshua helped her out of the sleigh and she held onto his hand as they made their way through the crowds. It was early evening now and it seemed as if the entire county had descended on the Christmas fair; families shared the space with young couples and groups of teens. The fairground rides were thronged, Christmas music played through the speakers and the stalls were doing a bustling trade. It was completely unlike New York at Christmas, but there was something endearing about the friendly, homespun nature of the event and, as they stopped to watch a local band, Rebecca couldn't help moving to the music, her foot tapping out the rhythm, her body swaying, Joshua's arms around her waist.

'Hey, you can move,' he murmured into her ear. 'Did anyone ever tell you that you should be a dancer?'

'Funnily enough, it has been mentioned once or twice,' she told him, turning round to link her arms around his neck, drawing him into the dance. 'You're not too bad yourself.'

'This is nothing; you should see me air guitar when the right song is on.'

'Is that right?'

'Oh, yes. I have been known to clear entire dance floors, especially when I skid across on my knees. My children don't find it in the least bit embarrassing.'

'I'm sure they don't. Especially not when they were teenagers.'

'Especially then.'

'Well, I for one would love to see you air guitar.'

'Maybe later, if you are a very good girl.'

'I promise.'

Their gazes held and her breath hitched in her throat at the sheer naked desire she saw in Joshua's eyes: desire, appreciation and, more attractive than either, liking and amusement. She leaned in for a brief kiss, loving the simplicity of whatever this was between them. Around them, people were continuing to sway and dance and she joined in, letting the beat of the drum, the bass guitar, thud through her, not worrying about grace or beauty, just enjoying the music and the moment, wanting to hang onto it for as long as she possibly could.

CHAPTER EIGHT

JOSHUA PULLED UP his planning document once again, but his brain refused to engage with the text and numbers on the page. The cabin felt quiet, too quiet. Thanks to Rebecca's help, the work had been completed quicker than he had dared hope for, but now that it was at an end she no longer showed up at ten, fresh from her morning class, heading straight to the coffee pot before throwing herself into whatever task needed doing.

He missed the company. He missed her. Now, if he wanted to see her, he had to text and suggest an activity or that she come over. Which was completely normal, especially when they had only known each other for a few weeks. But even so...

He was used to her being there. Sometimes quiet, intent on what she was doing, sometimes singing along to the radio in her tuneful voice, but there. It was odd to miss her presence when he had been alone for so long.

But he had work to do and he knew she did too, that she was planning to review her board papers and she'd set up some calls with her staff. 'I know I'm technically on vacation,' she had said. 'But it's too long to go without checking in at all.'

They both pretended they didn't know that she'd been checking in every day. He liked her commitment, her passion for her work. That it wasn't just something she did but something she lived and breathed.

He also liked it when she let go. He couldn't get over the way she had got into the music the other night, dancing as if she were lost in the beat, her eyes shining, the bulk of her coat and scarf transformed by her musicality. By the end of the set there had been quite the crowd around them, watching and applauding her, and Joshua had felt proud to be associated with her, to be the man spinning her round, the man she flung her arms around, the man she had kissed.

The man who had spent the last two nights barely sleeping, tossing and turning in his suddenly empty-feeling bed.

This was no good; he wanted to get this document finished so he could discuss it with

Marco over the holidays. It was time he took a step back from the chain as a whole, not resentfully or reluctantly but because it was Marco's turn to take the reins and because he, Joshua, had another passion project. That was what he'd been missing. Turned out he'd needed this time away, time working with his hands, to realise it.

But just because he needed to work now didn't mean he couldn't plan something fun for later. Joshua grabbed his phone and sent a quick message.

Looks like a perfect evening for stargazing tonight. Fancy it?

He didn't have to wait long for her reply.

I would love to.

As predicted, it was a perfect night. Joshua showed up at Rebecca's door around five, a flask of hot chocolate and a couple of cinnamon buns in his rucksack for when they reached the viewing spot on the other side of the lake. Rebecca opened the door already prepared for the chill of the evening in her ubiquitous white puffer jacket, snow boots, hat, scarf and gloves. She eyed the rucksack dubiously.

'I thought we were going for a walk, not a serious hike?' she said.

'It's always good to be prepared.'

'Moose spray, bear spray and flash flares?' she teased. 'Okay then, let's go.'

It was the most natural thing in the world for Joshua to take Rebecca's hand as they started to walk around the lake. It wasn't the largest of lakes, about half a mile across and a couple of miles wide, each cabin having enough land to guarantee privacy although with neighbours close enough if needed.

The lakeside path was open to the public, but most people didn't know it existed, which meant it was often only used by those who lived there and on a cold night like tonight Joshua knew he and Rebecca were practically guaranteed to have it to themselves. They set off in the opposite direction to Joshua's house, the cabin next door to Rebecca closed up and dark, shutters across the windows. As predicted, the stars shone brightly in a cold, clear sky with the moon so bright they barely needed the torches Joshua had brought with him just in case.

'This was a great idea,' Rebecca said after

a few minutes. 'I've been inside all day. I could do with both the air and the exercise.'

'Me too,' Joshua agreed. 'I think I finally got the bulk of the business plan down, but I must be getting old and my brain tired because that took far longer than expected.'

Rebecca laughed. 'Excuses, excuses,' she said, squeezing his hand. 'There's nothing old about you, Joshua Pearson.'

'Tell that to my kids,' he said rucfully. 'I'm sure they think I'm some kind of dinosaur.' It was why he wanted the plan to be perfect. At this point he was only going to show Marco—and Joshua was the CEO after all. He didn't need Marco's approval or permission. But he wanted both, not because he was Marco's father but because he wanted to know his idea was objectively a good one.

'You're barely fifty,' she protested. 'Plenty of men don't even become fathers until they're your age.'

'True, I do have friends with several children still at the toddler stage. I don't know how they have the energy. Each to their own, but I admit that, although it might not have been planned, I'm glad I had mine early.'

'You didn't consider having more?'

'Oh, we considered it, discussed it more than once. Gabi was only twenty-four when

Chiara was born, most of her friends were nowhere near having their first then, let alone their second. When they did start to have babies a few years later she had moments of feeling broody. And we had more money then, a house with a spare room, we both had flourishing careers. But, in the end, we just didn't feel we could go back to sleepless nights, all the baby paraphernalia. Everything was working out and we didn't want to rock the boat.'

Of course, barely a decade later the boat had not just been rocked but capsized by Gabi's diagnosis.

'I'm glad we didn't,' he said thoughtfully. 'It was hard enough when Gabi got ill, when she died, with Chiara still at school and managing her grief and mine, and helping Marco as much as he allowed me to. He was so closed off, I worried about him endlessly. If I had also had to look after a small child or two as well, raise them without a mother...' He shook his head. 'I'm just not sure I could have been a good enough mom and dad in that situation.'

Rebecca squeezed his hand. 'I think that if you *had* been in that situation you would have dealt with it by giving them all the love and security they needed and that you would have done an amazing job with them.'

'I appreciate you saying that. But although there are many things I wish I'd done differently, having more children isn't one of them.'

'Like what?'

Joshua exhaled. 'I knew travelling was Gabi's dream, one she passed on to Chiara, so although I thought Chiara should finish college and travel after, I supported her decision to drop out. But at the same time I wonder if I should do more to encourage her to settle down. I worry about her, where she's heading, what she'll do with her life. It's all very well travelling in your twenties but she's in her late twenties now and there's no sign of her choosing a career. She can't just go from place to place, job to job indefinitely. If Gabriella was here, she would know exactly what to say, to advise and how to say it—she and Chiara were so close. And I know Marco threw himself into work rather than work through his grief, just like I did. I wish I'd encouraged him to talk about his feelings more, to take some time out. It's all very well me concentrating on nothing but work, but Marco hasn't ever really let loose. And I wish I'd known to cherish every moment Gabriella and I shared. Not to wish a single moment away.'

Her hand tightened on his. 'The fact that you have those regrets shows what a good husband and father you are, and I'm sure the children know that you've done your best. Not long till they're here now; you must be so excited.'

'I am. I know it might seem ridiculous, a man of my age being so excited about Christmas. But it's just been so long since we were together again, been a family. I promised Gabriella that we would always spend Christmas together if we could. The last couple of years it felt like I let her down when we were all scattered.'

'From everything you've told me about her, I would bet that would be the last thing she would think or say. I think she would appreciate how much you've done to keep your family together and what an amazing job you did on the cabin, making sure this year is perfect.'

'I hope so.'

'I know so, and I think in your heart you do too.'

They carried on along the path in silence. Joshua hadn't talked so much about Gabriella for years. Not unless he was with the children or her family. It made so many people uncomfortable, talking about someone who had died, and yet by talking about her, keeping those memories alive, sharing who she was with someone new, it meant Gabriella was still here somehow. Rebecca's empathy and interest and gentle questions had helped him in ways he hadn't even known he needed. Thanks to this friendship, this burgeoning relationship, he was finally ready to move on because he knew now that doing so didn't mean forgetting Gabriella or betraying her, but that she would always be with him, tucked away into the corner of his heart that would always be hers.

'Thank you,' he said, and she looked at him in surprise.

'For what?'

'For listening, for understanding. You're an easy person to talk to, you know that? A good friend.'

'I hope so. I try to be a good friend, a good boss, a good mentor. Not to be thoughtless and selfish.'

He laughed. 'Those are the last words I would ever use to describe you.'

'They're exactly how Ivan describes me— and that's when he's tempering his language.'

'Your ex-husband should watch his mouth.' His lips tightened. He would like to say a few choice words to the man who had caused Rebecca such pain.

But Rebecca shook her head. 'He has cause. If you were him you might agree.'

'I don't believe it.' Joshua instinctively knew to tread carefully. 'I don't think that anything you do or did could diminish the liking and respect I have for you.' He meant it. Every word. 'I said the other night that I wouldn't press you to confide in me, but if you want to talk about it, I'm here.'

They walked on for a little longer, Rebecca unsure whether to say anything more or change the subject. But for the first time she did want to look back at her marriage and she instinctively knew she could trust Joshua to listen objectively. And if he did end up judging her, then surely it couldn't be as harshly as she judged herself.

'I was never the kind of girl to dream about getting married,' she said at last, and Joshua gave her a quick reassuring look. 'My sister Jennifer is only a couple of years younger than me. She always loved dolls and dressing up, talked about *when* she got married, not if. When she hit her teens, she even started to keep a binder full of dresses and venues and hairstyles, the lot, so when did she get engaged in her early twenties she knew exactly what kind of dress, what kind of wedding, what kind of reception she wanted. She had it all planned out. But for me, honestly, getting married wasn't something I ever thought about. All my energy, my focus was on my career. Getting into the Academy, getting taken on by the company, making soloist, making principal, becoming the best dancer I could be, they were my goals.'

'That's understandable. I hope the world's moved on from thinking marriage is every woman's destiny.'

She squeezed his hand. 'I hope so too, but not in my experience. As soon as a woman hits her late twenties people start asking if you're with anyone, is it serious, as if that's all that matters. I wasn't anti-relationships, I dated a reasonable amount, although my hours were never conducive to a normal dating life. And when those relationships ended I was sad, of course, but I soon distracted myself with work.'

'And look at the career you had,' Joshua said. 'That focus and singlemindedness paid off.'

She nodded. 'Exactly. I don't regret any of it. I was happy…really happy throughout my twenties and thirties. Fulfilled and driven and challenged. As for children, that's not something I thought about either. I never got broody; it's not that I don't like babies or children, I do, but I never wanted to take the time out from my career to have them myself. I do my best to make sure we are a family-friendly organisation, that any dancer who does want to combine a meaningful career with motherhood or fatherhood can, but when you're in the studio all day and dancing late at night it's difficult to do it without a lot of help and a very understanding partner. And, of course, there are the changes to your body—dancers' bodies are tools and pregnancy changes that tool. I've seen some women come back stronger than ever, I've seen others struggle to combine their competing priorities and leave the profession early. But for me it was never a problem because I was never in a serious enough relationship for the subject to come up and my biological clock just wasn't ticking in that way.'

'Not everybody wants to have children,' Joshua said. 'One of my sisters chose not to. She prefers to put that energy into being the best aunt she can be—she always says, much as she loves them, handing them back at the end of the day is her favourite part. All her nieces and nephews adore her.'

'Mine don't know me, and I am sorry about that. I'm not a good aunt, or a good sister or a good daughter. I know I don't share their interests and they don't understand mine, but I've realised that I have never really tried to bridge that gap. I wish I knew my nieces and nephews better.'

'It's not too late.'

'No, that's something I've been thinking about a lot. It's not.' Maybe her family felt as excluded from her life as she felt from theirs. There was only one way to find out.

'And you don't regret not having children now?'

'I don't, I really don't.' As she said the words she realised how true they were. 'What I love is seeing the children I know grow and flourish. To come across a young dancer with potential and to see that potential re-alised. To mentor young students through the Academy and welcome them into the Com-pany or see them accepted into other com-panies, or other careers if that's what they choose. This New Year's Eve, Freya—a tal-ented young dancer—is going to debut as the Sugar Plum Fairy. She first came to my at-tention as a child in the party scene in *The Nutcracker* when I was dancing Sugar Plum. I mentored her as a dancer, and then as her director over the last four years. Watching her succeed gives me such happiness. Watching them all succeed, whatever success looks like for them, makes me happy. I don't regret any choices that enabled me to pour my focus into bringing on the next generation.'

'I think that's laudable. I really do.'

'Thank you, but society can be judgemental about women who choose not to have children. Ivan didn't understand it; he thought it was selfish of me. Maybe it was.'

'Maybe Ivan should have focused on all the wonderful things you have achieved instead.' Joshua's voice was tight and Rebecca fought the urge to lean in to him.

'It wasn't all his fault. That's what I've come to understand over the last few weeks. Turns out sanding and painting gives you a lot of thinking time.'

'How long were you married?'

'Seven years. I met Ivan when I was about to turn forty.' Rebecca took a deep breath. Her marriage was something she'd done her best to avoid thinking about. Reliving it, even in conversation, made her chest tight and her throat seize up. She was glad of the reassuring grip Joshua kept on her hand, of the dark that enabled her to speak, that they continued to walk under the stars as she spoke.

'He's a film producer, a successful one, outgoing and confident and used to getting what he wants. We met when he produced a film with a scene set in a theatre; I was employed as the dancer on stage in that scene. He was on set that day and we got talking and as we wrapped the scene he asked me out for dinner.' She looked up at the moon, remembering that first date, how cherished and special she had felt. 'He's very charismatic, and I guess he swept me off my feet. That wasn't something I was used to. I'm usually pretty level-headed, used to an equal kind of relationship, but Ivan was the bombarding-with-expansive-gestures type and I fell for it, fell for him. I think it was as much to do with my approaching birthday as it was with him. Dancers have a sell-by date, and even though, as I was saying to you a couple of weeks ago, nutrition and better healthcare has extended that for many of us, there is something about turning forty that makes you realise at some point your life is going to look very different and I was avoiding that realisation. Ivan was the perfect distraction.'

They walked a little further as Rebecca thought back to that heady time of being romanced and wooed. 'Honestly, I didn't think he was serious. He was so all in it was almost a parody of courtship. When he would make statements about our future I'd laugh because it seemed so insane. I think I just as-

sumed the relationship would peter out once
he was back in LA and I was in New York.
But I completely underestimated him.

'After a few weeks we were conducting
a heady romance from opposite sides of the
country. It was easier for him to come to me
because of my schedule, and so he'd fly in
late on Friday and be waiting for me after that
evening's performance with a huge bunch
of flowers. He said my apartment was too
small.' She grimaced. 'That should have been
a warning flag. I love my apartment. I saved
for it, bought it with money that I earned, fur-
nished it with love. But Ivan has very different taste; he thought my vintage finds quirky,
my décor too colourful. He said he felt claus-
trophobic there so he would rent these huge,
expensive hotel suites, take me out to dinner,
treat me like some kind of special princess.
And it was a lot of fun. He knew everybody,
moved in a very glamorous, moneyed scene;
we had a really good time.'

She felt a lightening in her chest as she
said the words because it *had* been fun in
those first few years; it was easy to look back
and feel that she'd been foolish to fall for the
glitz and glamour, but of course she'd enjoyed weekends at lavish beach houses in the

Hamptons, being treated to trips on yachts, the tickets to exclusive events.

'As a principal dancer I was used to being invited to a lot of things, mixing with a variety of people from very wealthy philanthropists to other artists; it wasn't as if I wasn't used to a certain lifestyle, but Ivan lived on a completely different level. Those first months, the first year with him was like a fairy-tale. I had worked so hard for so long that it almost seemed as if I deserved to be part of that world for a while. But I never thought of it as something permanent.'

'Did you love him?' Joshua asked and Rebecca thought long and hard. It was a question she'd asked herself many times over the last few years.

'I thought I did,' she said after a while. 'But I didn't really know him, and he didn't know me, so how could it have been love? But I was just completely dazzled by him and how much he wanted me. So much so that when he proposed after six months I said yes. We got married six months later, after just a year together, even though we were rarely in the same place. It was the most impulsive thing I have ever done.

'Ivan thought he knew what my future should be. He thought retirement was round the corner, that I should move to California, that we could try for children, that I would become the perfect film producer's wife. He wanted a wife who knew how to make small talk, how to chat to important people, who had an interesting back story, who could be poised and glamorous and fit into designer clothes. I basically ticked all his boxes. And somehow, in those first days, I didn't stop to think whether he ticked mine. The thing is, I never told him that I could never see myself in that kind of life, that I wasn't even sure I wanted children, that I didn't want to be a trophy wife, that I wasn't ready to stop dancing yet. I was never honest with him, or myself, I just kept putting my retirement off, even after we were married. That's what he won't forgive me for—what I can't forgive myself for. That deception.'

'You strike me as a very upfront, honest person. It's hard to imagine you deliberately misleading anyone.'

Rebecca grimaced. 'It was self-deception. I knew when Ivan talked about me moving to LA I felt uncomfortable, that I disliked how he dismissed my feelings about moving, that I resented that he wouldn't consider relocating to New York. But, of course, I thought my dancing career was near its end and I didn't know what I wanted to do next. And here was this handsome, successful catch of a man wanting to make a life for me, a life many women would do anything for.'

'But you didn't retire?'

'No. When I agreed to marry him, I told him I wanted one last season. Then one of my favourite choreographers was asked to create a new ballet for the company. We had always worked well together and he decided to create the main character for me, so of course I couldn't retire just then. After that I felt in such good shape I decided to do another season, although Ivan made it clear he was unhappy. I loved Ivan—at least I thought I did, and I did love being with him, but I loved New York and my life there too. I liked visiting LA, but I just couldn't visualise myself there.' She sighed. 'By then we'd been married three years and I think we both knew we'd made a mistake but were too stubborn to admit it. And so we just kept limping on, he mostly in LA and me in New York. I think I really realised we were in trouble when I didn't want to tell him when I applied for the Artistic Director post. I told him I was applying for the experience, that I had no chance of actually getting it—and when I did get it my first thought was, "What will I tell Ivan?"

But it didn't occur to me not to take it. I'm surprised we lasted another couple of years.'

'So, what happened?'

She swallowed. There was no hiding from her contribution to the breakdown of her marriage. But she knew she had to finish the tale. 'A couple of years ago Ivan came to New York for a premiere of a work I'd commissioned and he was in a bad mood all evening. Back at the apartment he said that we really needed to think about children, that at forty-six it wasn't going to be easy for me and that if we needed to consider IVF or adoption then we needed to get started and it was time I joined him in LA so we could start to be a family. And you know, that wasn't unreasonable. I'd had five years in New York he hadn't planned for. But he could see I wasn't keen. We had a terrible row. He told me to admit that I had no intention of leaving New York, of having children, and I realised he was right. I didn't. When I finally said it, it was as much a shock as a relief.' She paused, remembering the clarity that had struck her as she had told him that no, she didn't want the life he did. 'He was so angry, said such bitter things, and I deserved every single one of them. I had strung him along, just as he said, denied him the life, the family, he'd wanted because of my own ambition, my inability to compromise.'

She couldn't forgive him for holding up the divorce for two years just to punish her, and she couldn't forgive the headlines and insinuations and the nasty publicity he'd whipped up against her. But she understood why he had wanted to make her pay because she had put his life on hold and put her own wants and needs before his. What kind of wife, what kind of person did that make her?

Joshua didn't say anything for a few long seconds, but his grip on her hand didn't ease and she clung onto that comfort. 'I can see why he was disappointed and upset,' he said at last, 'but didn't he know you at all? Why did he want to marry someone with your ambition and talent and turn you into a boilerplate Hollywood wife? Surely there were hundreds of women in LA who'd fit that bill? Marrying someone then wanting to change them is the most foolish thing any of us can do. You may not have told him in words how you wanted your life to be, but your actions could not have been clearer. If Ivan had properly loved you then he would have compromised, rather than forcing you to choose between your career and the life he wanted.'

Rebecca stopped and turned to look at

Joshua. Was that really what he had taken from her story? It was similar to Anita's take, to things other friends had said, but she expected them to be on her side. That was their job.

'Yes, but I could have…'

'He married a dancer at the pinnacle of her career, a career only achieved through sheer talent and hard work, who turned that career into something new and successful. He should have celebrated that, supported it, not resented it. Maybe you should have called it quits a lot earlier, that's true, but one thing I've learned about you over the last four weeks, Rebecca Nelson, is that you don't give up very easily and you don't like to fail. Sticking to a difficult marriage seems very on trend to me. But I think you should forgive yourself.'

She stared up at him, hope mingling with shocked surprise. 'You don't think I'm a terrible person?'

'I think you're a brave person who did her best to make the most of a bad situation. That's all any of us can do. We all make mistakes, Rebecca. All we can do is learn from them and move on.'

She could feel her mouth wobble, her throat catch, her eyes burn. She never cried, but this unexpected understanding almost undid her. She stopped and turned into his embrace, tears falling freely, and as she cried, some of the pain and guilt began to finally ebb away.

CHAPTER NINE

JOSHUA HELD REBECCA CLOSE, battling the myriad feelings swirling within him. Anger at her ex, who had wanted to take a remarkable woman and turn her into a trophy wife, pride at Rebecca for keeping her self-worth throughout, sadness that her marriage had never been a true partnership but a battleground. Tenderness for the brave woman weeping in his arms, tears he suspected she was shedding for the first time.

And, chief amongst those emotions, desire. It was inappropriate in the context—he was offering comfort not intimacy—but she was pressed so close. He could trace the strong, lithe lines of her back beneath the thick coat, feel the softness of her breasts against him, her breath on his neck, her touch on his shoulders. He wanted her, not at some point in the future, but now.

'You both wanted different things,' he said

after a while. 'That's not a crime. You couldn't find ways to be honest with each other or yourselves and that's sad but all too common. You held onto a dying marriage for far too long, but that's because you're not a quitter. But none of this makes you a bad person, Rebecca, it just makes you human.'

She raised a tear-stained face to him. 'Being here, with you, hearing your stories about family traditions, it's made me wonder if I have been missing out, if Ivan was right in saying that my ambition ruined everything. I have no Christmas traditions, barely any photos that aren't of me dancing. Did putting my career before family mean I did miss out?'

'Was Ivan suggesting he roll back on his work commitments? I thought not,' Joshua said grimly as Rebecca shook her head. 'Raising children is a joint commitment, no matter how you co-parent.'

'I guess so.'

'I know so. And you do have family traditions. I've heard you talk about what's going on at the theatre right now, the rehearsals and the dinner you have after the first stage call, the party you put on for all the children and the gift exchange on Christmas Eve. I've seen the cards and flowers and gifts that keep being delivered to you from your friends and colleagues. I've heard you on the phone to dancers having crises of confidence and your empathy and practicality as you coach them through it. You made a family, Rebecca. That's a huge achievement. I think,' he added, carefully searching for the right words, 'I think it's healthy to look back at your marriage and see what went wrong, to learn from it. But you don't need to blame yourself.'

'Ivan blames me.'

'Because his plans didn't work out. You may not have told him out loud what you wanted, but from I've heard you made it clear. He chose not to understand; that's on him.'

'You don't think I'm selfish, too ambitious, a workaholic?'

He continued to choose his words carefully. 'I think you need aspects of those traits to get to where you have, as a dancer and director. Anyone successful does. I do. Marco does. It's what they are tempered with that's important. You temper yours with kindness, generosity, humour, tenacity, thoughtfulness. That makes you strong and successful and there's nothing wrong with that.'

Rebecca didn't answer for a long while, her expression serious under the moonlit sky. 'Thank you,' she half whispered finally. 'Thank you for seeing me.' She rose onto her tiptoes and kissed his cheek lightly, almost chastely, before cupping his face in her hands, her touch sending warmth shivering through him. 'You're a good man, Joshua Pearson.' Another kiss. 'And a very sexy man.' A third. 'Can we go back to the cabin?' She pulled back and looked at him, her face unflinchingly open and honest. 'I'm tired of taking things slow.'

There was no mistaking her meaning.

The last thing Joshua wanted to do was take advantage of Rebecca's weakened emotional state, but there was nothing weak in her stance, in her expression, in her voice; instead she was the strong, proud woman he so admired.

'We can do whatever you want.'

'I want to go back. With you.'

'Come on then,' he said, his voice hoarse. 'Let's turn around.'

It was quicker to retrace their steps than to circumnavigate the rest of the lake. Neither spoke on the twenty-minute return journey, not to comment on the stars blazing overhead, or the beauty of the moon and how it reflected on the ice; instead they strode through the snow, hand in hand, gloved fingers entwined. Anticipation beat a steady rhythm through Joshua's veins. Gone was the doubt, the fear of moving on, in its place a certainty that tonight, at least, this was exactly where he needed to be, she was exactly who he needed to be with.

They still hadn't spoken when they reached the cabin and Joshua unlocked the door, ushering Rebecca in. They took off their hats and gloves, discarded coats and boots and walked into the living space. Joshua turned on one lamp and walked over to the stove, already laid waiting, and lit it. Rebecca stood near the sofa as he coaxed life into the fire, her head high, still, waiting.

'Wine? Beer? A soda?' Joshua offered but Rebecca shook her head.

'Just you.' She stopped, bit her lip. 'If you still want to?'

If he still wanted to? What kind of question was that? He reached her in two swift strides and tilted her chin up so he could look into the hazel eyes, drink in the perfection of her oval face, dramatic cheekbones, the full lips every part of him ached to kiss. 'I want to. But I'm happy to keep taking things slow if you want to. There's no rush, Rebecca.'

'There's less than a week until Christmas,' she said, and he grinned.

'It's now or never, you mean?'

'I mean we don't want to take it so slow it never happens at all.'

'No, we don't.'

'So what are we going to do about it?'

'I think you should kiss me. No, wait. I'm a modern woman. I can kiss you.'

Her kiss was soft, warm, inviting, and Joshua responded in kind, slow and sweet and languorous, holding her lightly, not wanting to rush this. All doubt had gone, there was no guilt, this was where he wanted to be, needed to be.

Slowly, slowly, he walked her back until they reached the long, comfortable couch and he sat, gently manoeuvring her onto his knee without breaking the kiss, tangling his fingers in the silk of her hair, caressing the curve of her neck, acutely aware of her fingers splayed against his chest, the warmth burning through the fabric of his sweater as he dropped kisses along her jaw, finding the hollow in her throat and hearing her gasp as he tasted it before returning to the intoxicating full softness of her mouth.

It was a long time since Joshua had made out on a couch—a long time since he had made out like this at all—but his body, his hands, his mouth all still knew exactly what to do. Layers of clothing were discarded, some smoothly, some with laughter and interruptions until they were lying full length on the sofa in just their underwear. There was no embarrassment or awkwardness, just trust and murmured endearments and sensation as she whispered kisses along his jawline and down his neck, her hands exploring every inch of his sensitised torso, while he caressed and tasted every dip and curve from the dimples in her shoulders to her navel, before making his way up to small but perfectly formed breasts, shadowy in the fire-lit dark. She gasped as he circled the rosy tip with his thumb, the sound shuddering through him.

The last scraps of clothing were somehow discarded, the sensation of being fully skin to skin almost overwhelming. Joshua raised himself onto his elbows and looked down at Rebecca, her hair spread behind her, eyes glazed with a desire for him that almost undid him.

'I don't have any protection,' he said, voice raw. 'I could go to the store or...'

'I'm tested and protected,' she told him, looking at him openly and with trust. 'If you don't want to take my word for it there is other stuff we could do.'

'Stuff?' he teased, gently shifting his weight and seeing her eyes darken with the sensation. 'I am interested in seeing what this stuff might be but right now, if you're sure...'

'More than sure.'

With a Herculean effort he pushed off her, smiling at the small cry of distress she gave and extended a hand.

'Comfortable as this new sofa is, I can't help thinking that we might be better off with a bed?'

'You do?'

'Better springs for a start,' he said as he pulled her up. 'I'm fifty, I need all the help I can get.'

'Well, in that case, Joshua Pearson...' She wound herself around him and he found her mouth in a searing lingering kiss. 'Let's go and test those springs.'

It took Rebecca a few minutes to figure out what was different. This wasn't her luxurious guest suite, but Joshua's bedroom, newly repainted in the soft sage she had chosen, with bronze accents picked out in the bedding and blinds. He was no longer lying next to her, and she rolled over, clutching the sheet to her, squinting against the golden winter sun slanting into her eyes. The enticing aroma of coffee wafted up, mixed with the scent of baking pastries, and Rebecca realised how hungry she was.

Of course they had skipped dinner.

She rolled a little further, burying her head into her pillows, not knowing whether to be embarrassed by the memories that assailed her or to take each one out and relive it. Memories of firelight playing on naked skin, of soft murmurs and tantalising kisses, of sweet caresses and delicious touches. It had been so long since she had been with a man, so long since she had found herself so undone, laid bare in every way.

No, not too long. It had never been quite like that before. Never so intense, so intimate, with such trust. How could she face him? It was as if he knew all her secrets.

At the sound of footsteps coming up the stairs she quickly scanned the room for clothes, remembering with heated cheeks that hers had been discarded in the living room. She pulled the sheet up even higher and waited, a little nervously, for Joshua to come into the room.

If he had similar reservations, it wasn't obvious. He was showered and dressed in sweatpants and a T-shirt that clung rather nicely to the torso she had explored so intently last night, carrying a tray with the coffee and a plate of pastries on.

'Good morning.'

'Is it?'

'Good or morning?'

'Both.'

'Morning, just. Good? It is from where I'm standing.' His smile was knowing and her cheeks heated even more. 'No regrets?'

'No.' Because she didn't have any. 'You?'

'Only that whole go-slow nonsense. Now I know what we were missing out on, I'm wondering what we were waiting for.'

'I don't know.' She managed to meet his eye. 'Anticipation can be part of the fun.'

Joshua set the tray down on the bedside table and sat down on the bed next to her, reaching out to take her hand. 'It was fun.'

Was? Fun? But of course, it was just a fling. Two lonely people in need of healing who had been thrown together. A special time, a memory she would always cherish, but this wasn't either of their real worlds.

But it didn't mean she wanted it to be a one-off. 'Was?' she repeated.

'Well, hopefully it will still be fun.' His eyes glinted with mischief—and desire, a desire for her that made her stomach swoop and all thought leave her brain. 'I didn't want to presume you'd be interested in a repeat performance.'

Rebecca reached out to grab the neck of his T-shirt and pulled him close. 'Presume away, Mr Pearson, presume away.'

'If my lady insists.'

If last night had been long and languorous, an intense exploration, a sounding out of what worked, likes and sweet spots, this morning was applied learning. Joshua's kiss was incendiary, sending her pulse speeding up and her nerves crackling with anticipation as he slid his hand up her ribs, clever fingers sure and knowing as he cupped her breast, his thumb circling her nipple as she writhed against him.

'Your skin is like velvet,' he murmured against her mouth, his other hand stroking her inner thigh. Rebecca could hear her breathing speed up as he teased and nibbled. All she could do was grip his shoulders and pull him tight against her, legs wrapped round him.

'You taste like honey and wine and all things nice.' Now he was kissing her neck, his hands continuing to explore. 'I just want to kiss you everywhere.' He pulled back and looked down at her, brown eyes gleaming with a mixture of desire and teasing intimacy. 'Would you like that?'

He dropped a kiss onto the top of her breast and Rebecca moaned.

'What was that?' He turned his attention to her other breast and she shifted against him, the friction driving her wild.

'Yes,' she gasped, beyond pride or reason. 'But then...' And with satisfaction she saw his eyes darken with anticipation. 'But then I may just return the favour. And,' she added recklessly, 'I'm going to make you beg.'

He laughed, low and dark, and her stomach tumbled. 'We'll see who begs who,' he promised and as he took her mouth with his she lost all thought for a long, long time.

Showered and kind of dressed in one of Joshua's sweatshirts and a pair of Chiara's old leggings, freshly washed hair tied back, Rebecca sat on the sofa, eating a now cold pastry and sipping reheated coffee, her whole body at once aching and yet alive, a similar sensation to when she'd finished a show. She scrolled through her phone, checking emails, tapping out those which only needed short replies while trying to summon up the energy to either return to her own cabin or collect her laptop. Her PA had sent a proposed schedule for the New Year and she did her best to make sense of it from the tiny screen, looking for tweaks and amendments.

'You look a million miles away,' Joshua commented. He was at the table, busy on his laptop. Rebecca looked over and smiled.

'Finalising the schedule. It's like a really complicated jigsaw involving lots of different people, places and budgets.'

'In what way?' He looked properly interested, which was one of the things she liked best about him.

'Well, there's the theatre itself. We share it with the opera company and we have some visiting companies too, although that's more usual in the summer. I need to put on a varied programme that caters to enthusiasts, experience seekers and tourists, but one that also marks our status—so a mixture of classics, newer works and commissions of brand-new work. Any choreographers for next year have already been contracted, of course, but I always have to be several seasons ahead. Then there are dancers. Have any of mine have commitments we know of? Do I have enough guest artists? Are we touring, and if so, where? Are we commercially viable?

Classics make more money than new work, partly because there's less cost associated, partly because you attract a wider audience like tourists, families, experience seekers. A good *Nutcracker* run will carry smaller companies for the whole year.'

'You have to be coach, manager, financial officer, marketing person combined. That's impressive.'

'Well…' She couldn't deny the glow of appreciation that lit her up at his approbation. 'There are people doing all those jobs, of course. They make recommendations and we come to a consensus but the final decision about what goes on the stage, when and who dances it is all mine.'

'And you love it.' It was a statement and she nodded.

'I didn't think anything would replace dancing but I do. I get the same adrenaline rushes, the same thrills from seeing a successful performance I was responsible for putting on—with a lot of other people, obviously— as I did from being the one on the stage. Not exactly the same, but as satisfying.'

'When you talk about the company, your dancers, your plans, you light up like one of those children coming away from Father

Christmas the other night. It's one of the things I most like about you.'

'Really?' For a moment she wanted to ask if he was just saying it, if he wanted to give her reassurance after her vulnerability the night before.

As if he sensed her thoughts, Joshua nodded. 'Really. It's a rare quality: that commitment, that passion. Embrace it, be proud of it.'

Rebecca nodded, unable to find the words to reply.

After another ten minutes staring at the tiny numbers she tossed her phone aside, realising she really needed to get her laptop, and wandered over to Joshua. 'What are you up to? I've seen a lot of furious typing and number crunching, not the actions of a man condemned to the golf course. Anything interesting?'

'I hope so.'

Rebecca sat her cup down on the table and slid into the seat next to him. 'Is this those vague plans you've been hinting about? Want to talk it through?'

Joshua ran a hand through already dishevelled hair. 'I'm the CEO of the Grand York hotel chain, the board answer to me, and yet I feel as nervous as when I first suggested expanding out of New York to my father.' He laughed. 'Nervous and determined and fired up.'

'That's great.' She nudged him with her elbow. 'So?'

'Well, the Grand York specialise in city boutique hotels. They are welcoming, family friendly but luxurious, using older buildings where possible to add character, and always in the heart of the city.'

'And...'

'The inn you stayed at in the town is for sale.'

'Ah.'

'It's one of a small chain throughout New England; there are seven locations altogether. I want to buy the chain and create a Grand York Inn brand, something smaller, more bespoke than the hotels but still offering the luxurious, family-friendly experience we are famous for.'

'Inns seem like quite a departure from what you do already. The scale and feel are so different, and they tend to be rural as well.'

'Absolutely. The economy of scale is very different, the staffing, décor, activities: everything. And I can see my board suggesting we stick with what we know, keep expanding into Europe, look at other US cities—

which would be a valid response. The truth is that even if they don't get behind me, I could push it through—I'm the owner after all—or I reckon I could even do it on my own, but I'd rather do it as part of the family business with Marco's buy-in. It gives me a distinct new project to sink my teeth in and it means I could spend more time here, which would be a bonus. I've lived in the city all my life. I want more country air in my lungs. You gave me the idea, actually.'

'Me?'

'When you said I could turn the cabin into a B&B. I know it was a joke, but it got me thinking *what if* and I realised that actually I wanted something smaller, more bespoke, away from the city and mine.'

'So you'd be up here, what? Half the year?'

He shrugged. 'No idea, but a lot more than I am now. This time up here, away from the city, it's been rejuvenating. I'd forgotten how it feels in Vermont, the fresh air, the scenery, nature all around me, hiking and skiing on the doorstep. I've lived in New York all my life, it's my home and I love the sound and smells and pace, but I love it more when I can step back for a time. And that's what I want to offer with these inns. A step back.'

And that settled it. Rebecca had also loved this time away, completely understood what he meant about the rejuvenating qualities of the still Vermont winter, but her life was in the hustle and bustle of New York. Her life and, more importantly, her work. Not that there was much differentiation between them.

Joshua understood that, liked it, respected it, and that had gone a long way to healing some of the wounds in her heart and soul. But he was planning a life that took him away from the city. This wasn't the start of something new; it was a moment out of time. A rare moment, something to cherish, but he was only just moving on from his wife and she was just beginning to recover from her marriage. Neither were in the right place emotionally or physically to try and be anything more. It was good to get that clear in her head.

'I hope I get to stay in one of your inns.'

'I'll make sure you get an upgrade.'

'Joshua…' Rebecca hesitated, unsure how to frame what she needed to say. 'Thank you for everything—your company, listening to me, the ski lessons, showing me Vermont, all of it. I feel like I've made a new friend, hopefully a friend for life. I hope we will still get to see each other sometimes. I'd love you to be my guest at the ballet some time, for us to grab a coffee occasionally.'

He turned to look at her, his usual expression inscrutable. 'I'd like that,' he said after a while. 'Friends sounds good.'

'But,' she added, hoping he didn't think she was regretting the night before, 'we still have a few days until Anita and Trudie and your children arrive, and I was thinking that I don't want to ruin this friendship but…' She smiled at him, allowing suggestion into her expression, her tone.

'But?' he teased, and her smile widened.

'Guess.'

'If you're thinking Friends with Benefits, then I agree, and if you're not can I ask you to consider it? Because I really, really enjoyed last night and this morning. We seem to be good together. It seems a shame to stop when we've only just begun.'

She wanted to lean over and kiss him until her whole body was filled with nothing but him, but instead she stuck out her hand. 'I agree to the benefits clause while we're still here. It seems a mutually attractive proposition.'

'Always the businesswoman,' he teased,

enfolding her hand in his. 'Any more clauses or sub clauses to add, Ms Nelson?'

Now she couldn't resist leaning in for a kiss. 'I'm sure I can think of something.'

CHAPTER TEN

'REBECCA?' JOSHUA WALKED into his neighbour's cabin and looked around. The seasonal decorators Anita employed for every occasion had been in the week before and the cabin was now decorated in a tasteful cream, silver and crimson theme from the imposing tree to the lights and decorations. The cushions had been recovered with Nordic-style Christmas covers, matched by the throw and rug, and the table was already set, towering candles in the middle. Enough champagne, mulled wine and punch to intoxicate the whole town had been delivered the day before and were cooling in the wine cellar, and a side of smoked salmon and other tasty treats chilled in the fridge.

His own home wasn't so different, also filled with food and drink; Anita and Trudie might have ordered their provisions from an upmarket deli in New York, but Joshua was more than happy with the produce he'd sourced locally. Trying all the local producers was as much research for his business plans as preparing for Christmas dinner. But, in his enthusiasm, he'd completely over-catered as well as adding several new decorations to the already full box.

His chest tightened. In just a few hours both his children would be here and his family would be complete—and it was. They would all always miss Gabriella but over the last few weeks he knew he had finally started to envision not just carrying on without her but living without her. Renovating the cabin, contemplating a new business venture, one that would take him out of the city for weeks at a time, allowing himself to want Rebecca, to sleep with her. These were all momentous steps.

And it looked as if he wasn't the only one taking steps this Christmas. Both Chiara and Marco had messaged with ETAs and a heads-up that they weren't alone. He had no idea whether they were bringing friends or lovers or how many people they had with them, but there was a guest room and camping beds in the attic if needed; they'd manage, it was Christmas after all. It would be good to have the cabin full of people celebrating.

So it was a good thing he'd over ordered and bought those extra presents and stockings.

'Rebecca?' he called again.

He heard the sound of her tripping lightly down the stairs and a few seconds later she crossed the room to drop a light kiss on his cheek. To his surprise, she was still in her yoga pants, hair up in a knot, no make-up, looking class-ready not going-out-ready. As far as he knew, Anita had planned to come up before Trudie to whisk Rebecca out for lunch and a business chat. By the time they returned his children would be here. Their time together was nearly at an end—which was why, rather than stay with him last night, Rebecca had insisted on returning to her cabin and own bed and why he hadn't dissuaded her.

Joshua knew now he was ready to date again—who knew, maybe one day even love again—but his children didn't, and he didn't know how they would react. He didn't want to spoil their Christmas in any way. Besides, he and Rebecca weren't really dating. She had her life and he had his, and they didn't need or want to complicate this friendship by adding expectations on it they couldn't keep. She'd made that very clear and he saw the wisdom of her choice.

He would miss her, though. An occasional

coffee didn't seem enough after such an intense few weeks. They might have known each other for a short time but she had become very important to him.

Rebecca squeezed his hand as she stepped back. 'Hi, I wasn't expecting you.'

'I rang the bell, but you didn't answer so I tried the handle. Do you mind?'

'Of course not.' But her smile was wan. 'I was in the shower.'

'I just wanted to see if you had any milk? I'll replace it today, but Marco will be here in an hour and I managed to spill mine.'

Rebecca gestured to the fridge. 'We had several pints delivered yesterday with the rest of the groceries. Take as much as you want and don't worry about replacing it; in fact, take anything you can use that's perishable. Trudie and Anita aren't coming.'

'What? Why?' She was trying her best to hide it, but Rebecca was clearly disappointed. 'I thought they were looking forward to it. Invitations have gone to the whole neighbourhood…'

'Flu,' she said succinctly. 'They're laid up in bed feeling very sorry for themselves. They're in no fit state to travel, let alone host or eat or drink all this rich food.'

'Oh, no, poor Anita and Trudie.'

'I know. I wish there was something I could do.'

'And poor you.' There would be no business lunch and dinner with friends, Christmas Eve party or lavish Christmas Day celebrations. 'I know how much you were looking forward to seeing them.'

'I do feel fed up, but obviously it's far worse for them. I've had my break, but they've been working so hard. And I think they both feel pretty wretched, poor darlings.'

'What are you going to do?'

'I'm used to working over Christmas, I have since I was first a mouse in *The Nutcracker*, so spending it alone is not really a big deal. A fire, a good book and some of that salmon and I'll be fine. My surroundings are a lot more festive than usual.' She looked around at the lavish decorations and the fourteen-foot tree decorated to within an inch of its life. 'Although it does seem overkill for just me!'

'Look, spend Christmas with us,' Joshua offered impulsively but as soon as the words were out he knew they were right. The kids had both brought company, why shouldn't he? 'I'd love you to meet the kids, you'd be very welcome.'

'That's really sweet, but I wouldn't want to intrude.'

'Of course you wouldn't be intruding. I've already got at least two unexpected guests so one more will make no difference—and it looks like you'll be providing half of the feast.'

'Well, I guess I can't eat all that salmon on my own.'

'So you'll come? Great!' He wasn't just being polite. Rebecca had been such an important part of his life over the last few weeks—so integral in helping him take the steps he had—that it felt right she celebrated Christmas with him, got to see the traditions they'd discussed in person, spent some time with the kids. He was sure they would like her and she them.

After all, it wasn't as if they would just never communicate again after the festive season. Friends she had said, and he hoped she meant it.

'If you're sure.'

'Absolutely. Marco gets here first—he's arriving in time for lunch—and Chiara at some point this evening. Why don't you head back with me now?'

'Looking like this? No, you need some time with your family without worrying about extra last-minute guests. Why don't I join you for dinner later?'

'And what are you planning to do all day?'

'I...'

'Work?'

'Probably.'

'This was supposed to be a fun day.'

'Starting with a business lunch,' she reminded him, and he laughed.

'With your best friend who just happens to be your publicity manager and agent.'

'Not so much that any more,' she admitted. 'There are far fewer modelling possibilities for a woman of forty-eight and far fewer promotional tie-ins for an Artistic Director than there were for a Principal Ballerina— no one wants dolls or a series of books from me any more. Not surprisingly, that honour falls to our current popular dancers. Most of the publicity I do promotes the company and is handled inhouse, but I couldn't have managed the fallout from the divorce without her.'

'So get dressed and come over to have lunch with us,' he suggested. 'We won't choose the tree and decorate it until tomorrow, but I thought a walk this afternoon and then I get out the old board games. I know how much you love to win...'

'But Joshua, seriously, you have been so looking forward to spending this time with your children; the last thing you want to do is worry about entertaining me. I'll be fine, honestly.'

'They're bringing guests. Don't make me look like the sad loner in front of my kids.'

'Oh, well, in that case, I am the one doing you the favour.'

'Always,' Joshua said softly, and leaned in to kiss her gently. 'Always.'

He knew prolonging the physical relationship between them was probably foolish, and he didn't want his children to know that they were more than friends, not because he was ashamed in any way but it would come as a shock to them. Rebecca had made it clear that this was a short-term fling and he saw the sense in that, so why put Marco and Chiara through that shock? But kissing her, touching her, felt so right, it was going to be harder than he'd imagined saying goodbye at the end of the holidays. Having her spend some time with him and the kids might help recalibrate the relationship, make it easier to say goodbye when the time came.

'This is going to be a great Christmas,' he told her. 'Just wait and see.'

Rebecca was used to challenging situations, but she had to muster all her courage to walk over to Joshua's an hour later. She'd dried her hair and put it up into a loose bun, dressing in bronze velvet jeans and a loose gold sweater, keeping her make-up to a minimum. She wanted to look collected and professional, like the kind of woman who would be friends with Anita and Trudie, not the woman who had spent the last week sleeping with the father of the two strangers she was about to meet.

She rounded the corner and saw a black, expensive-looking SUV parked next to Joshua's car. She took a deep breath. One of his children—Marco, she guessed from what Joshua had said earlier—was here already.

Children! They were adults. Adults who had adored their mother. Who were no doubt protective of their father. What would they think of her? Would they guess she and Joshua were more than friends? Would they disapprove?

She shook off her misgivings. What did it matter? She was returning to her real life soon. If they mistrusted or disliked her, well, she would never see them again. Squaring her shoulders, she knocked on the door and it was almost immediately opened by a beaming Joshua.

'Come in, come in. Come and meet Marco and Eleanora.' He ushered her through, barely giving her time to change into the slouchy flat boots she had brought with her and take off her coat and scarf. A tall young man with a distinct look of Joshua sat on one of the new sofas, holding the hand of a pretty young woman with gorgeous auburn curls. 'Marco, Eleanora, this is Rebecca who has been staying at Anita's cabin over the last few weeks. Rebecca, my son and his fiancée.'

Fiancée? Was that new? She was sure Joshua had said Marco was single. She looked enquiringly at Joshua and he nodded. 'Hot off the press. I had no idea they were even dating, but I couldn't be happier—Eleanora is one of my most talented managers and has been busy opening the hotel in Rome, but more importantly I already love her like a daughter. I couldn't be more delighted.'

'That's wonderful, congratulations to you both.'

'What's more...' Joshua's beam was even wider, if such a thing was possible. 'I'm going to be a grandfather!'

'Oh, that is lovely news! I am so happy for you all.' The news made small talk a little easier as wedding and baby plans offered an easy topic of conversation, as did the changes to the cabin.

'Dad said you were responsible for a lot of

the work and all the decoration,' Marco said, and her cheeks heated.

'I hope you don't mind…'

'Not at all. I was busy apologising in advance to Eleanora for the state of my room the whole way here and wondered if we should book into the inn, but then Dad showed us all that you did. You've achieved miracles. Thank you.'

'I like to keep busy and needed a project so really I'm the grateful one for the opportunity. I enjoyed the challenge.' She could see his brown eyes, so similar to Joshua's, appraising her shrewdly. He was clearly no fool.

Joshua had pulled together a light buffet style lunch and as they ate the two Pearsons and Eleanora discussed how the hotels were doing over the festive season and plans for New Year celebrations across the chain, before Joshua moved on to questioning his son and his fiancée about how things were going at the hotel in Rome and where they should expand next. Rebecca had little to add to the lively conversation, but it was interesting to see Joshua in this new light—focused, incisive, on top of all the figures and facts. His assessment of himself as the ageing patriarch was way off the mark, as Marco and Eleanora were clearly pleased with his approval.

It was a timely reminder that she had only known Joshua for a few weeks and that there were huge swathes of his life she had no knowledge of. The laid-back tour guide and renovator was just a small part of his whole.

'So, Dad, Eleanora agrees with me that *Die Hard* is a Christmas film,' Marco said as he collected the dirty plates and stacked them on the counter. 'Please, no sappy romantic comedies on Christmas Eve. I vote for *The Muppet Christmas Carol*...'

'No votes necessary. *The Muppet Christmas Carol* is a staple,' Joshua said firmly.

'And then *Die Hard* and *It's a Wonderful Life*.'

'We have to have at least one romantic comedy,' Eleanora objected, and Marco rolled his eyes.

'Do we?'

'Absolutely, and it's very underhanded of you to start lobbying your dad before Chiara gets here. Christmas Eve isn't Christmas Eve without at least one romantic film, isn't that right, Rebecca?'

'I usually work Christmas Eve, so I don't really have an opinion,' Rebecca admitted. 'But if I was to sit down and watch something Christmassy it would probably be a performance of *The Nutcracker*.'

'Don't you ever get bored of it?' Eleanora asked curiously.

She shook her head. 'I know how it sounds, but no. I'll watch a different version if I was watching for fun—I love to see all the different interpretations from different choreographers—but no, I am never bored. The second I hear the overture, that's Christmas for me. I suppose it's because I danced in it every Christmas since I was little, as a mouse, a party guest, then a snowflake or a featured role, then Clara and finally the Sugar Plum Fairy.'

'And you always worked Christmas Eve?'

'Always. The day after Christmas as well.'

'So what do you usually do for Christmas? When do you get to see your family?'

'I don't usually, as there isn't time. But that's part of the job.'

'I guess.' But Eleanora didn't look convinced and the conversation returned to the forthcoming wedding. As she put the plates away, Rebecca realised how little she had in common with these family-orientated people, her choices and life so different to theirs.

With lunch tidied away, they headed out for a walk, skates in hand for those who fancied the extra exercise. The walk was peppered with reminiscences and plans for the future, and Rebecca began to feel more and more on the outside. She was neither past nor future, although Joshua did his best to draw her in. It was a relief to step out onto the ice and move, her usual way of dealing with emotions.

It was dark by the time they returned to the cabin and Joshua lit a fire and drew the curtains, turning the large space into a warm, cosy room. Rebecca's offer to help prep dinner were waved away and so she sat with Eleanora, watching Joshua and his son work together, joking, teasing and competitively chopping vegetables, both showing off the chef tricks they had picked up in the hotel kitchens.

'Joshua is a wonderful father,' Eleanora said, her hand straying to her stomach. 'I know Marco will be the same.'

'You've known them long?'

'All my life. Joshua and Gabriella were such young parents, so fun, we all idolised them. It was devastating when Gabriella died; all I could do was sit and listen and try and help Marco through his grief. It's a real testament to how close they are as a family that they came through it together. I feel so lucky to be part of the next chapter, to add my own traditions to Marco's and to be able to create a Christmas for our own child next year.'

Rebecca could only nod. Her time with Joshua had been such an idyll out of time and space it was discombobulating to remember that it wasn't real life or anything like it. This time next year he would be running the inns and welcoming his grandchild to the cabin for Christmas, while she was in New York in her rightful place at the head of the company.

Joshua set his knife down at the sound of tyres outside, his eyes alight with happiness. 'Is that Chiara?'

Rebecca hung back, feeling even more out of place as the family—including Eleanora—rushed out to meet the car. They were soon back, bearing a beaming young blonde woman with Gabriella's smile, clutching the hand of a handsome, expensively dressed man of around the same age.

'You and Eleanora?' she was saying as they trooped in. 'I didn't suspect a thing, but it makes perfect sense! I am so happy for you both. I can't wait to be an aunt. I am going to spoil him or her rotten, I warn you now. But where are my manners! I was so happy to see Eleanora I forgot to introduce Evan. Dad, Marco, Eleanora, this is Evan Kim. Evan, this is everyone. He rescued me from a bit of a hole. I'll tell you all about it later, Dad,' Chiara continued. 'But without him I wouldn't be here. He offered me work and a chance to come home—I know I could have called and you would have helped, but you'd already sent me money and I just couldn't ask for more.'

'Nice to meet you, Evan.' Joshua offered the younger man his hand. 'Thank you for taking care of my girl.'

'Oh, she's the one taking care of me,' Evan replied with a look of such tenderness towards Chiara, Rebecca was surprised to feel tears prickle at the back of her eyes.

'Evan is already part of my family so it just feels right he's here with us. I am so excited to show him a real Pearson Family Christmas.' Chiara slid an arm around Evan's waist and leaned in against him. 'He asked me to marry him, and I said yes. I know it seems really sudden and that we haven't known each other for long, but it feels right, Dad.'

'Oh, sweetheart, when you know, you know,' Joshua said. 'I am the last person to lecture anyone on how they fall in love and when. It's what you do with that love, how you nourish, it that counts. Congratulations, both of you. I am very happy for you and for Marco and Eleanora. I think this calls for champagne—Eleanora, I know we have some sparkling water but it doesn't feel very festive.'

'Don't worry. I have some sparkling elder-flower at the cabin; I'll go back and get it.' Rebecca was on her feet and shrugging into her coat before anyone had a chance to react, slipping out into the cold night air with re-lief, glad to have the space, the silence, time to gather her thoughts, Joshua's last words ringing in her ears, tumbling through her thoughts.

It's what you do with that love, how you nourish it, that counts.

She didn't know if she had ever really loved Ivan, but she did know that she hadn't nourished what they did share, and nor had he. In fact, Rebecca had never nourished a romantic relationship, although she did her friendships. Had never been as certain as Marco and Eleanora, Chiara and Evan of the rightness of another person. True, the two couples in the cabin were at the beginning of their journey together. Of course they were glowing; right now the world was full of pos-sibilities.

But Joshua also believed in love, and he was the veteran of a twenty-year marriage. One he admitted had had its rough patches, times when competing priorities had put a strain on the couple. But they had still nourished their relationship, so much so it had taken a decade for him to move on.

Was she even capable of loving like that? Maybe she had always seen romance as a distraction from her real goal, partners not a support but a hindrance, demanding time and attention she didn't choose to spare. Was she doing that again? Ruling out anything more with Joshua because she didn't want to feel as if she had to choose between work and him?

To her surprise, her eyes were heavy with tears and Rebecca blinked them back determinedly as she retrieved the elderflower soda. She was tired, that was all, and sad about the changes to her plans, realising her winter idyll had neared the end, nothing more.

She really liked the open, easy affection between the Pearsons, the pride in Joshua's eyes when he looked at either of his children, the affection and respect he received in return. She'd liked how excited he was showing Marco around the cabin and how they teased each other in the way only families secure in their love for one could do so.

She wanted to be part of it, not just an observer. Over the last few weeks she had been the one Joshua had teased, had treated with affection, had focused on. It wasn't that she was jealous, not at all, she liked to see him so happy. It was just…

It was just she hadn't been ready for it to end. She wasn't ready.

She returned to the cabin with the elderflower fizz in hand to be properly introduced to Chiara and Evan. Like her brother, Chiara was complimentary about Rebecca's work on the cabin—but like him she was also clearly curious about Rebecca's long stay at the cabin next door and wondering about the friendship between Rebecca and her father.

The cabin felt festive and full of love, a family playlist playing through the speakers, Chiara dancing as she set the table, aided by Evan, Eleanora lending a hand in the kitchen, but once again Rebecca's offer to help was waved away. It was all very clear; she was a guest, they were family, the cabin she had helped plan and renovate no longer her and Joshua's private space but their home. And that was just as it should be.

'So, Marco, when's the wedding going to be?' Chiara asked.

'We just want something quiet,' Eleanora said, her hand caressing her stomach.

'And soon. Maybe Valentine's?' Marco smiled at his wife-to-be.

'You romantic.' Chiara grinned at her brother. 'Who would have thought it?'

'It's not the wedding that counts,' Joshua said. 'It's the intent. Your mom and I got married at City Hall on a Thursday afternoon…'

'We were very young…' Marco said dramatically.

'Money was tight,' Chiara added.

'But we had each other.'

'And love.'

'That's enough, you two.' But Joshua was laughing.

And at that moment Rebecca knew. She wasn't feeling out of sorts because her Christmas plans were ruined or because she was uncomfortable intruding on this family Christmas. She was disturbed because everything had changed. She didn't just like Joshua as a friend or value him as a lover. She was falling in love with him.

Falling? No, it was too late for that. She had toppled headlong.

She couldn't pinpoint when, but now she'd realised it was blindingly obvious. She was in love with him, that was why she had spilled her deepest fears and regrets, why the sex had been so intimate and all-encompassing. It shouldn't have come as such a surprise; he was kind and insightful, funny and intelligent, and he saw her, really saw her.

He was also enjoying his first family time in years and she couldn't intrude where she didn't belong any longer. What if someone guessed? What if she gave her feelings away? He had been happy with the decision that they stay as friends, he was only just considering the possibility of embarking on a future relationship with someone other than his wife. She shouldn't be here being needy, distracting him. He needed this family time.

She pulled out her phone and flicked through her work emails, desperately trying to think of an excuse to leave before dinner. She would have to head back to New York as she'd find it hard to resist Joshua if she were just next door. Rebecca waited until Joshua left the busy kitchen and headed towards the small hallway and followed him through.

'Hey, you.' His smile was so bright it almost hurt and, despite herself, she could feel an answering smile tugging the corner of her mouth. 'What do you think of my kids? They're pretty great, aren't they?'

'They're wonderful,' she said honestly. 'I am so happy for you that you get this time with them and with so much to celebrate.'

'I'm a lucky guy.' His gaze sharpened. 'What's wrong?'

'Nothing. It's just I had a message from work and there's been a minor crisis. I just feel like I've left my deputy to take on too much recently and I can't ask her to deal with this too. Then there's Trudie and Anita. I hate the thought of them alone and sick over Christmas. I can't tell you how much I appreciate your offer to let me spend the season with you, but I really feel I need to head back to the city. Good thing we haven't had that toast yet.'

Joshua's penetrating gaze made her feel as if every almost-lie was exposed. There was a small issue with cast changes, thanks to seasonal colds, and she would feel better dealing with them in person rather than over the phone. Plus she really did want to check on her friends. But neither were the real reason for leaving. She made herself smile at him as she put on her coat and slipped on her boots.

'Have a wonderful, wonderful Christmas.' She stood on her tiptoes and kissed his cheek. 'Say goodbye to the others, I don't want to intrude.' And that right there was the essence of her withdrawal. 'Goodbye—and thank you for everything.'

And with that she slipped through the door and headed out into the cold, leaving Joshua in the warmth.

CHAPTER ELEVEN

JOSHUA STOOD STARING at the door for several minutes, trying to process what had happened. Rebecca had been unusually quiet all day, but then he had never seen her in a larger group and the family had been so full of each other she probably had hesitated to intrude. He hoped she hadn't felt unwanted or in the way. Something about her tone hadn't rung quite true.

But then again, she had always been intending to travel back to the city with Anita and Trudie the day after Christmas. She'd just brought her dates forward. It was understandable under the circumstances. Joshua couldn't deny he was disappointed, that he'd been looking forward to sharing his Christmas traditions with her, but he understood.

Slowly he returned to the living area. The music still played and Chiara was still dancing, laughing up at Evan in a way that made

Joshua's heart ache with happiness. His mercurial, restless daughter seemed so happy and settled with Evan, who clearly adored her. Gabriella would have been delighted and he knew she would have instantly welcomed Evan into her heart and the family. Who knew where the pair would end up? Evan's own family were in Singapore but the young billionaire had been living in Bali and travelled all over the world. It would be nice if they settled close to New York, but if not, well, Joshua wouldn't mind regular trips to Bali!

Eleanora and Marco were laughing together in the kitchen, his son filled with a happiness and tenderness Joshua had never seen before. The couple made perfect sense. He was just surprised it had taken them so long to see it. And a baby! Fifty might seem young to be a grandfather but he couldn't wait until the cabin was filled with children again.

There was a lot to celebrate.

'Rebecca has asked me to pass on her apologies,' he said as he walked across the room. 'She needs to head back to New York earlier than expected but she enjoyed meeting you all.'

'That's a shame,' Eleanora said, brows drawn together thoughtfully. 'She seems nice.'

'Mom used to take me to see her dance.'

Chiara collapsed into a chair. 'I didn't get a chance to tell her, it felt a bit fangirlish, but honestly, the way she turned. I wanted to be her at one point. Do you remember when I took ballet lessons, Dad?'

'I bet you were cute,' Evan said, and she laughed.

'It was all about the accessories for me. I liked the tutu but I didn't have any talent, sadly.'

'She's worked really hard on this place.' Marco strode across the room to perch next to his sister. 'How did you manage to swing that, Dad?'

'She's had a tough year and wanted a project—and the cabin was too much for me alone in the time I had to get it ready.' Joshua was very aware that he was working hard to keep his tone light. 'It was very serendipitous that she ended up in the cabin next door. I would never have got everything done without her help.'

'I like the way it's still our cabin, not all fancy and designer. It has the same comfortable feel but fresher.' Chiara's smile was full of memories. 'You even kept our artwork on the wall, although I think I had about as much talent for art as I did for ballet. I really like the photo of Mom and me in my room too.'

'That was Rebecca; she had a real sensitivity for the history of the cabin.' Joshua was aware that his voice was gruff and both his children were watching him keenly.

'You've spent a lot of time with her recently. You'll miss her.'

'I've enjoyed getting to know her, it would have been a lonely few weeks otherwise, but I have you now. And we have a Christmas to celebrate. How are those steaks looking, Eleanora?' Briskly, Joshua changed the subject. He would miss Rebecca, but for now he was going to concentrate on being with his family. After all, he'd been looking forward to this moment for so long.

That night they ate the steaks and played board games, every one of them fiercely competitive until at times Joshua could see the teenage Chiara and Marco instead of the adults they had become, as they accused each other of cheating, all the while cheating outrageously themselves. It wasn't until he was lying alone in his bed that he had the opportunity to realise how much he'd missed Rebecca throughout the evening. It was selfish of him—he had his family with him, and she had her own life to return to—but true. They had spent so much time together over the last four and a half weeks that she had become part of his life without him realising.

But this wasn't either of their real lives. She was upfront and unapologetic—as she should be—about the claims her job made on her time, on her life. The luxury of leisure was unusual for both of them. It was just a lovely coincidence they had been able to share it.

But he missed her.

Christmas Eve dawned bright and cold and the five set out early to find the perfect tree, traipsing through the pine forest that surrounded the lake, Joshua warning as he did every year that they needed to carry it home and not to go too far from the cabin. As always, Chiara begged for a tree so big it would barely fit in the cabin and, as always, Joshua persuaded her into something bigger than he had planned but smaller than the tree she had set her heart on. Both Evan and Marco offered to be the one to fell it, but Joshua liked to keep this honour for himself, for now at least. When Marco's child was old enough to help pick, he would hand over the axe to Marco, and to Evan too one day, but he wasn't ready to relinquish the patriarch role just yet, although he was glad to have two strong young men to help carry the tree, Chiara also shouldering her share although they as one banned Eleanora from helping, despite her protests that she was pregnant not bed-bound.

Decorating the tree was his favourite part of Christmas and this year was no different. The scent of hot chocolate and gingerbread filled the room as the family rifled through the box Joshua had sorted out earlier and hung the decorations on the newly installed tree. It took a long time as every bauble was exclaimed over, its story relayed to the new family members, just as he had relayed them to Rebecca. Amongst them were the baubles he'd picked out at the Christmas fair and as he handed a wooden carved sleigh to Chiara his chest tightened, remembering the feel of Rebecca's head on his shoulder as they had driven by the frozen river, the way she had swayed in his arms as the music took hold of her.

'This is my favourite day of the year,' Marco said as he carefully hung a wooden painted stocking he'd made at school onto a low branch. 'Even last year when we were all in different places, I had Chinese take-out Christmas Eve, then watched *Die Hard* with cookies and warm milk. Some things shouldn't change.'

'*Die Hard* is not a Christmas movie.' Chiara put her hands on her hips. 'Evan, tell my brother.'

'Well...' Evan prevaricated, and they all laughed as Eleanora stepped in.

'I'm with Chiara, but I am prepared to concede *Die Hard* if you concede one romcom.'

'As long it doesn't involve fake British accents and castles.'

'Oh, no.' Eleanora wagged her finger at her fiancé. 'You don't get to make terms.'

'In fact I am looking for something with nothing but fake British accents and as many turrets as possible,' Chiara chimed in.

The teasing and laughter continued as they drank the hot chocolate and ate the gingerbread, poring over the takeaway menu and dissuading Evan from flying in an order from his favourite Chinese restaurant in New York.

'The local restaurant is very good,' Chiara assured him. 'Obviously it's nothing like the food we ate in Singapore, but I think you'll like it.'

As Evan conceded to her, Joshua realised the truth he'd been hiding from. His children weren't just grown up in name, they were grown up in every way. They no longer needed him; they were forging families and memories and traditions of their own. It was inevitable, but he hadn't expected it just yet. He left them still munching the snacks and went upstairs to unearth the stockings to hang by the fire and the box of gifts to put under the tree.

The gifts and stockings were in the spare room closet, where on top of the box were five gifts in wrapping paper he didn't recognise. The biggest was addressed to him from Rebecca, the other four to Marco, Chiara, Evan and Eleanora. When had she sneaked these in here? It was typically thoughtful.

'Look,' he said as he carried the box into the living room. 'Rebecca left these, wasn't that kind?'

'Very kind.' Chiara took the box out of his hands and set it on the floor. 'Are you okay, Dad?'

'Me? Of course.'

'It's just,' Marco said, 'you seem a bit subdued.'

'It's hard to get a word in edgeways,' he tried to joke, but none of the four faces gazing at him anxiously smiled. 'I am more than fine. We're together; that's all I wanted.'

'Wanted,' Chiara repeated slowly. 'Past tense. What do you want now?'

'Tell us about Rebecca.' Eleanora smiled

at him. 'You've spent a lot of time together, I know.'

Honestly. Did these ridiculous youngsters think he was pining?

'We have. As you know, she's been very helpful over the last few weeks.' That should shut them up.

'Did you do anything but paint?' Marco's face was all innocence.

'Well, I taught her to ski. And we hiked on Thanksgiving. Went to the Christmas fair. Skated. Cooked together…'

'So a lot of time together then. That's good, she seems really nice.' Chiara picked out the presents Rebecca had left. 'And thoughtful.'

'She is. She's had a tough year; her divorce just came through and it was a drawn-out affair. She came up here to get away from some nasty headlines and have a break.'

'So you set her to work?'

Joshua glared at his daughter, who gave him a bland smile. 'She insisted. Said she just couldn't sit and do nothing so I made a deal; I'd show her some of what Vermont has to offer in return for help here. You know, it's three years since I last headed up here and I have no idea why I stayed away so long. Being here has done me the world of good.' Good, a nice subtle change of subject.

'Maybe it wasn't the place, maybe it was the company.'

'Or both,' Marco added.

'We became close,' Joshua admitted. 'She's an extraordinary woman. Very strong, ambitious, determined. But I haven't, I mean we're not…'

'You lit up when she was in the room,' Chiara said gently. 'And the two of you created a home here. Together.'

'Her ex-husband wanted her to be someone she wasn't. For her to change her life to fit with him. She has a job that requires her to be in New York most of the time, to work seven days a week if necessary, and I'm looking at spending more time up here.' Joshua could feel himself getting frustrated. Not because he was having to explain himself to his children but because he could hear how weak his excuses were. 'We grew close. The closest I have been to anyone since your mother. But that doesn't mean it's some big love affair; it's just a holiday romance.' He looked at his children anxiously. Would they be upset? But instead they were both smiling, giving each other an *I told you so* look.

'And that's fine if that's all it is. But, Dad, if you have feelings, real feelings, for Rebecca, I think you should let her know.'

'Mom would want you to be happy, Dad.'

'If you two are happy then I'm happy.'

'You still have so much of your life ahead of you. Do you really want to spend it alone?'

At some point Evan and Eleanora had melted away and Joshua found himself sitting on the sofa between his children.

'I'm not alone.'

'You'll always have us.' Chiara snuggled in against him as if she were still a little girl. 'But, Dad, you gave us all the tools to be ourselves. You gave Marco responsibility and showed him how to be a good leader, you gave me permission to be free. You have given us stability and love and confidence, but we still found it hard to recognise love when it was in front of us. Well, it took some of us longer than the other...' She grinned at her brother. But for once he didn't retaliate.

'I *didn't* see what was right in front of me,' Marco admitted. 'I've known Eleanora all my life but I think I was scared of loving, scared of losing...'

'Losing your mother was the hardest thing I have ever experienced.' Joshua held his children close as the years melted away. 'But I wouldn't have given up one second of knowing her, loving her, even knowing the pain it would one day cause. Because it was worth it. She was worth it. I am glad you have found the courage to follow your hearts, both of you.'

'Then will you do the same, Dad? Do you love Rebecca? And if so, will you tell her?'

Did he *what*? Joshua almost laughed, the idea was so preposterous. No, of course he didn't love Rebecca! He liked her, admired her. Wanted her.

He liked the way she made him laugh, the easy conversation that flowed between them. He liked the way her brow crinkled when she was deep in thought, the way she lit up when excited. He liked her determination, her focus, her unabashed competitiveness and her joy when she accomplished something new. He liked the way she listened, her understanding and empathy.

He liked the way she was absorbed and fulfilled by her work, that it was a vocation which fulfilled her. He admired her talent and the drive that had taken her to the top not once but twice. He admired her fierce protectiveness of all the dancers under her care, how she wanted to give them safe spaces to enable them to be the best they could be. He admired the grace that imbued everything she did, from walking across a room to skating. He admired her understated beauty.

He wanted her in his arms, in his bed, by his side.

But did that add up to love? How did a man know? Last time it had all seemed so simple, youth wiping away doubt, inexperience wiping away questions.

'I...'

'It's okay if you love her,' Chiara said softly. 'We just want you to be happy.'

'There are so many reasons not to love her,' Joshua said slowly. 'I thought my heart died with your mother, and for a decade that was fine, I had no intention of dating again, but then I saw Rebecca standing by the side of the road and everything changed.'

'What would you say to Mom if she was here and you weren't?'

There was no doubt. 'If it had been the other way round, I wouldn't have wanted Gabi to be alone. I would want her to seize happiness. But Rebecca has only just disentangled herself from a disastrous marriage, one she rushed into and regretted ever since. The last thing she needs is to be swept off her feet again.' He stopped and considered. That was true, but he hadn't set out to fall for Rebecca, it had just happened. 'But then, he wanted to change her from the beginning, whereas I think she's perfect the way she is.'

'That's two obstacles you've sorted,' Marco said, a tremor of laughter in his voice. 'Go on.'

'Her life is bound up in her work. She's unavailable much of the time as she works evenings and weekends and holidays. She's bound to the city, whereas I want to spend less time there as I have a project of my own I want to pursue that will mean some travelling. But then again, it's the quality of time not the quantity, isn't it? We're not teenagers, we don't need to live in each other's pockets, we don't have children needing us to be in the same place.'

'Besides, it's the twenty-first century; we are always connected if we want to be. There are phones and texts and video calls when you're away,' Chiara said. 'Evan travels a lot, but that's no reason for me to give up on him. Okay, I will mostly travel with him, but not every time.'

'And I'll need to visit hotels all over the world,' Marco added. 'Eleanora knows that. And her job is pretty demanding too, long hours, weekends and holidays, but we'll make it work.'

'So no more excuses, Dad. Only you know how you really feel. Was this just a brief fling—and there's a sentence I never thought

I'd use to my own father—or something more?
And if it is something more, then what are you
going to do about it?'

'I love her.' Joshua looked at his clever,
perceptive children in shock. How had they
known before he did? 'I do. And I need to
tell her!' He jumped to his feet. 'I have to go.'

'Yes.' Chiara smiled at him. 'Go and bring
her back to spend Christmas with us.'

'My plane is only a few miles from here,'
Evan said as he emerged from the kitchen,
phone in hand. 'It's ready to take you to New
York and bring you back here. A car will be
here in twenty minutes.'

'You are going to be very useful to have
around.' Joshua squeezed his children close
one more time before getting up and clapping
the younger man on the shoulder. 'Thank you.'

'And, Dad?' Marco nodded at him. 'Good
luck.'

It wasn't until Joshua was halfway to the car
that he realised he had no idea where Rebecca
lived. Would he find her at the theatre? He
checked his phone—today's performance had
finished at four. Even with the gift exchange,
she was likely to have left by six. He could
call her, of course, but he had the sense that
what he had to say was best said in person.

What if she told him not to come? There was only one person who could help him.

He tapped out a message and sent it. He was in Anita's hands now. She'd sent Rebecca to him in the first place. He just hoped she would allow him to finish what she'd started.

CHAPTER TWELVE

REBECCA LOOKED AROUND her apartment and tried to summon up some festive spirit. After she'd got home last night she'd done her best to decorate, but her attempts looked puny compared to Anita's lavish display and Joshua's well-loved decorations. Her tree was small, the handful of ornaments sparse and her attempts to emulate the Pearsons by ordering Chinese takeout and lining up some Christmas films felt pathetic at best.

It wasn't that she wasn't happy to be home. She liked Anita's stylish cabin and adored the setting, but she loved her little brownstone apartment with its jewel-coloured walls and vintage furniture, the old playbills carefully framed on the walls along with memorabilia—the pointe shoes she had worn when she debuted Odette/Odile, a collage made from old costumes and leotards given to her when she'd retired from the stage, a tiara, pressed flowers from her first bouquet. It was her sanctuary.

And she had been overwhelmed by the welcome when she'd returned to the theatre the evening before, the sense of rightness, the knowledge that here was where she belonged. Never would she allow herself to leave it for so long again—although she had to concede that holidays were in fact a good thing and she would take more of them more regularly.

Of course she now knew she could work elsewhere for short periods of time if the opportunity arose. Memories assailed her of the snow falling gently outside the windows, Joshua frowning at his laptop while she watched morning class and took notes, coffee on the stove, soup in the slow cooker. But that was the past, not the future. She had taken one romance that should have stayed a fun memory and turned it into a disastrous marriage; she had learned from her painful mistake.

But if she was being honest with herself, she wasn't looking forward to spending Christmas on her own. She was rested, not exhausted, lonely, not in need of peace. Usually so happy with her own company, she felt decidedly flat. Maybe she would feel better after she'd made some phone calls, calls she was dreading but ones she realised were both necessary and overdue.

She poured herself a glass of wine and took it over to the big, squishy, emerald-green sofa and curled up, taking a deep breath as she stared at her phone, selected a name and pressed the call button. It rang for a few seconds before it was answered.

'Mom? It's Rebecca.'

'Rebecca? Is everything okay?'

The surprise in her mother's voice tore at her heart as she continued the conversation. Surely she should expect to hear from her daughter at Christmas. 'Yes, I'm good. Did you get the hamper? I was in Vermont. Yes, it was pretty, super snowy, I skied. Not bad actually, I'd like to go again. How is everyone? They're all with you? Staying for the holidays? That sounds amazing. Me? A quiet one, you know how it is. Yes, I know I'm always welcome, it has been too long. Maybe I can get over before the New Year. Yes, I'd like that too.'

It was a short but not uncomfortable conversation, followed by a couple of minutes with her father, who never was that chatty on the phone—or in any other sphere—and then, to her surprise, with her youngest sister, whose two daughters studied dance and, she said proudly, took after their aunt. 'They'd love to see a show, maybe come backstage, and if you do ever have the time to see them dance...'

Before she knew it, Rebecca was offering tickets and a tour for a few days' time, almost dizzy with surprise as the conversation flowed. Was she an outsider or had she made herself one? Had she subconsciously pushed her family away, both misunderstanding and feeling misunderstood? If so, here was her chance to put some of that right.

She rang off, realising she was looking forward to showing her nieces around, to entertaining her sister and her husband. Katy was eight years younger than Rebecca and by the time she had grown out of toddlerhood Rebecca was already spending every waking hour at the studio. She was only six when Rebecca had left home. It was no wonder they weren't close, but maybe there was the possibility of some kind of sisterly relationship in the future. She was determined to be a better aunt at least—and not only to those nieces and nephews who shared her interest.

She'd just made a first positive step.

But there was another call to make and she was a lot less optimistic about this outcome. She didn't expect him to pick up, half wondered if he had blocked her number, and her stomach clenched with trepidation as she heard the familiar voice.

'What's wrong?'

'Ivan? It's Rebecca.'

'I know. That's why I assumed something was wrong. I can't imagine any other reason you would call me.'

Rebecca squeezed her eyes closed. She deserved that, she supposed.

'No, nothing is wrong. At least...' She searched for the right words and in the end realised they didn't exist, she just had to say what was in her heart. 'I'm sorry, Ivan. I didn't ever intend to mislead you. Not when we got married, not a few years later. It was never my intention to hurt you.'

Silence. She took a deep breath. 'The truth is I am guilty of lying to myself and therefore to you. I thought that at some point I could be the wife you wanted, but I should have known myself better, I should have known that the life you offered me was never going to be the right kind of life for me.'

Still silence greeted her but she knew he was listening. Rebecca inhaled again, her stomach churning with nerves.

'However, this apology doesn't mean I accept all the blame, it doesn't excuse some of your actions. I don't like the way you treated me over the last couple of years, how clear you made it that you wanted to hurt me. And I certainly don't like your behaviour over the last few months, the briefing against me, the planting stories in the press, the way you painted me as the villain. Because of that it's been very easy for me to blame you for everything that went wrong, but I've done a lot of thinking and I know I had culpability too. But that doesn't mean I'm taking sole responsibility, Ivan. One thing I have realised is that you never wanted me as I am. I was never enough for you. You always wanted to change me, and that's on you.'

'What is this?' But he was still there, and he didn't sound angry, as she had half feared he would.

'This is me moving on, it's me accepting the mistakes I've made, yes, but also absolving myself of the mistakes I didn't make. We were together for a long time, Ivan. Too much of it we spent apart, and too much of it was bad. But we had wonderful times too, and I want to remember those. I want to remember that our marriage had some really good points and that, no matter how I felt over the last couple of years, there were many times when you made me really happy. I guess I wanted you to know that as well.'

There was a long, long silence. 'I was very happy too,' he said at last, his voice taut. 'Maybe you're right, maybe I did want to change you because I knew I couldn't hold onto you otherwise. Maybe I did allow my anger to influence my behaviour too much, especially recently. I'm sorry, Rebecca.'

Rebecca blinked back tears. She wasn't sure she'd ever heard Ivan apologise before and hadn't realised until she did how much she needed to hear it. 'Me too. I hope you're happy, Ivan. I wish you well.' It felt so freeing to let go of the anger and humiliation, to realise she didn't need to carry around the burden of guilt and regret any more. She'd moved on, she was ready to face her future, whatever it might be.

'Me too. Thank you for ringing. For saying that. Goodbye, Rebecca.' And then he was gone.

Rebecca sat back and picked up her wine, her brain whirring with all that had happened this evening, and over the last five weeks. She'd been changed more by her time with Joshua than she had by all her years with Ivan. She'd looked outside the life she'd made for herself and found things to embrace, had yearned for things she had never yearned for before: family and tradition and acceptance for who she was.

Yet maybe those things were possible, within her grasp. Now she had accepted how much of her emotional happiness and self-worth was bound up in her work, she had re-alised that she didn't need to feel guilty about her workaholic tendencies, that she received as much as she gave to her work. But she had also realised that it wasn't too late to open up her heart and her life to her family. And she was finally able to move on romantically too. Thanks to Joshua, she knew that not every relationship had to be a battleground. That she deserved more.

Her chest squeezed. Only she didn't want to move on. At least, she didn't want to move on with just anyone.

She wanted to move on with Joshua.

But it was impossible, wasn't it? It had seemed so at the cabin. But if she was open and honest about what she could and couldn't give and he was the same, did they have a chance?

Only... What if he didn't feel the same way?

There was only one way to find out—if she was brave enough to try.

She'd been brave enough to make the first

steps in reconnecting with her family, brave enough to finally draw a line under her marriage. Could she be brave enough to reach out for happiness too?

Not now. Not when he was celebrating with his family, the way he had been yearning to do. But maybe after Christmas she could arrange to see him, to try and be honest with him, no matter what came next.

Her buzzer rang, jolting her from her thoughts. Of course, her food. She put her wine down and walked through to the front door, trying to summon up an appetite for the feast she'd ordered in an attempt to feel Christmassy, pulling out some dollars for a tip.

Rebecca opened the door, money in hand and thanks on her lips, only to stand there stupidly and stare at the man who held a brown paper bag full of steaming food. 'What? Joshua? But…' The words just wouldn't come.

'I met the delivery guy on the doorstep and offered to take it off his hands. Very trusting in your neighbourhood, I must say. Maybe he was reassured that I knew your name.'

'It's my usual place; they deliver late after the theatre closes.'

What was he doing here? 'Where's Marco, Chiara, everyone?'

'Can I come in? The food is getting cold

and the bag is heavy.' His expression clouded suddenly. 'Do you have guests?'

'I was just being greedy,' she confessed, and he laughed.

'Then it's a good thing I showed up; it smells fantastic.'

The whole thing was ridiculously surreal, but somehow Rebecca found herself busying about, putting out bowls and chopsticks and spoons, filling water glasses and pouring Joshua a glass of the wine she'd opened earlier. While she set the food out, he wandered around the apartment, checking out the photos and posters on the wall, the vases and ornaments and other things she'd collected over the years, her books. It was a little cluttered by the minimalist standards of the interior design magazines, the colours not to everybody's taste, but she hoped he got it.

'This place is very you,' he said, picking up the musical box Anita had given her one Christmas. 'It shouldn't be, you dress in neutrals and you are very collected on the surface, whereas this is bright and full of emotion and sensation. But it's like the feelings you evoke. I can't imagine you anywhere else.'

Warmth flickered inside her. He did get it. Get her. 'Thank you,' she managed as she set out the containers on the kitchen worktop. 'Here, it's ready. Help yourself.'

'Great, I'm starving. The others were still bickering over the menu when I left.'

The most natural thing in the world would have been to ask at that point what on earth he was doing here, but Rebecca was suddenly shy and instead handed him a bowl and urged him to eat as much as he wanted. Her own appetite had disappeared and she nibbled on a piece of dim sum, her stomach in knots.

'So what have you planned for this evening?' Joshua asked as he took a seat at the table.

'I was going to watch a film.' She was too embarrassed to tell him that she had cookies in the cupboard and milk in the fridge for later, that she was emulating the evening he'd planned for his family.

'You know…' His tone was casual but he was watching her very closely. 'We have an evening of film-watching planned too. Why don't you come back with me and watch films with us?'

'How did you get here?' she burst out. 'How did you find me?' She was sure she'd never given him her address.

'I asked Anita. She made it very clear that she wasn't happy about handing out your details without your permission. I have been warned that if I upset you in any way she'll be after me, seasonal flu or not. And as for how? Let's just say Chiara's new beau is proving very useful indeed. If she doesn't marry him, I might. He lent me his private jet, calm as you like. I have to say I could get used to being the father-in-law of a billionaire.'

Rebecca couldn't put off the main question any longer. 'But why?'

'Because…' He put his bowl down deliberately on the table and she saw that he had barely touched the food either. That sign, that he wasn't as calm as he seemed, gave her strength she didn't know she needed. 'Because I didn't want to spend Christmas without you. In fact, I don't want to spend the New Year without you either, or spring or summer or fall. I'd like to spend all the holidays with you, and a great deal of the seasons as well. I've fallen in love with you, Rebecca.'

'But…' Even as elation and hope filled her, she was trying to think of all the reasons it was a bad idea. All the reasons that had come to her yesterday, the second she'd realised she was in love with him. 'But what about your children?'

'I don't know if you noticed, but they're very grown-up and the last thing they want to worry about is their old dad being lonely. They're the ones who persuaded me to come chasing after you on Christmas Eve. You know, I've always been a fan of Christmas Eve treasure hunts, only this year I'm searching for something for me, something that I hope isn't just for Christmas.' His smile was achingly tender as she jumped to her feet and paced the room.

'But my job is here, and you're planning to spend more time in Vermont.'

'Both these things are true, but we're adults, Rebecca. We don't need to live in each other's pockets, we can support each other from wherever we are. Vermont is not so far from here after all. You could come and work a couple of days up there when your schedule allows, and I'll still be here more than half the time and whenever you need support—I'm still the CEO of the Grand York. That won't change, I'm needed here. The only thing I really see as an obstacle is if you don't feel the same way. And if you don't, just say so. But before you do, I just need to tell you that I love you because you are you. I don't want to change you in any way, I don't need you to fit in with my life. I want to see you flourish and shine in all the ways that make you happy.'

Rebecca couldn't find any words. She just

gazed at Joshua, her brain churning. She could do this, she'd already made giant steps in taking responsibility for her own happiness and relationships this evening. She just needed to find the courage now, when it mattered most. 'I love you too.'

The light blazing from Joshua's smile heated her through as he jumped to his feet and strode over to her, cupping her face in his hands.

'You're not just saying that?'

'No, no, I do love you. I realised yesterday. That's why I left. I knew I didn't belong at the cabin, crashing your family's special time. I couldn't be there as a stranger and I didn't want to risk spoiling what we had, spoiling your Christmas by telling you how I felt. It all seemed impossible.' She couldn't quite remember why now.

'Nothing is impossible if we want it enough.'

'And I do. The first thing that struck me was how thoughtful you are, how kind. Well...' she smiled at him '...after I noticed how hot you are.'

'Naturally.' He grinned boyishly and she laughed.

'You seemed so laid-back, but I soon realised that that didn't mean you weren't focused and determined, only you didn't let those characteristics dominate your life. I love your big heart, how much you love and support your family, the effort you put into making them happy while supporting them for who they are. I love the way you make me feel, like I am enough.'

'You are more than enough.'

'And you are more than I ever dreamed. Or am I dreaming? Will I wake up and realise none of this is real?'

'I hope not. Because in that case I am dreaming too. Rebecca, I know you just left Vermont, but I would love for you to come and spend Christmas with me and my kids—and they would love for you to as well.'

'You're sure they won't mind?'

'Mind? They practically shoved me out the door.'

'Well, in that case, how can I say no?'

'But first…' her stomach tumbled at his wolfish grin, his eyes full of intent '… I have been wanting to do this all day.'

She rose to meet him in a kiss so tender it almost undid her, a kiss full of love and desire, a promise of happiness to come.

Rebecca was unusually shy as Joshua opened the cabin door and ushered her inside. It had taken a while to leave her apartment after the kiss escalated until she led him into her bedroom, their lovemaking unhurried and sweet, a consummation of their emotions. Afterwards she had packed an overnight bag and cleared away the uneaten takeout, her appetite still completely gone, her body too filled with happiness and desire.

But now she was here some of the certainty that had propelled her through the evening had gone. Did the younger Pearsons really want her at their family Christmas?

'You're back!' Chiara jumped up from the sofa and ran over to embrace first Joshua and then Rebecca. 'Don't worry, Dad, we saved The Muppets for you—and there are lots of leftovers if you're hungry. I am so glad you came back, Rebecca. Dad was very mopey without you.'

'Mopey?' She looked up at Joshua, whose eyes crinkled with laughter.

'Maybe a little.'

'Good,' she told him. 'Because I think maybe I was a little mopey too.'

Before she could catch her breath, Marco had taken her case upstairs and Chiara installed her on one of the sofas with a plate of food that Rebecca was now hungry enough to eat.

'I'm putting the cookies in to bake now,'

Eleanora said as she wandered in with the frozen cookie dough in her hand.

Chiara was right behind her. 'And then I'll warm up milk for those who want it, hot chocolate for the others.'

'The Muppets are ready to go.' Evan brandished the remote control. 'As soon as everyone else is.'

It was just a little noisy, just a little chaotic— and a whole lot perfect. As Rebecca sat back, Joshua by her side, she looked around at the transformed cabin, now ready for Christmas. The tree was up and decorated, including the decorations she and Joshua had picked out at the Christmas fair, the lights were all on and every shelf had some kind of Christmas ornament. The fire crackled and cast a warm light over the family as they took their seats, ready to fulfil this sacred Christmas tradition, Eleanora and Evan entering into the spirit of it just as she was.

There was an enticing pile of presents under the tree, including the ones she had left, and six stockings hung on the mantel. *Hang on, how many?* She counted again. Yes, six. Each was named, the battered, much-loved ones were Joshua's, Marco's and Chiara's, the new ones had 'Evan' and 'Eleanora' inscribed on them. How had Joshua got that done in time? His love for Christmas, for family tradition, for family itself, and his ability to include everyone in those, was one of the things she found most endearing about him. She looked at the last stocking and her breath caught; *Rebecca* was written in swirly gold letters.

This was going to be a perfect Christmas.

CHAPTER THIRTEEN

JOSHUA TOOK HIS seat and looked around the beautiful old theatre. Modelled on the great European opera houses, the auditorium curved gently, rising in tiers. Every one of the red velvet seats was full. The last *Nutcracker* of the season was a New Year's Eve tradition in many New York homes and, in true celebratory style, most of the audience had dressed up—and the Pearson party was no exception. He, Marco and Evan were dapper in black tie, Eleanora elegant in a draped pale gold and Chiara radiant in blue chiffon.

His gaze rested on Marco and Chiara as they laughed at some shared joke and his heart squeezed with love and thankfulness. *We did it, Gabi.* His job as a parent would never be done—and he didn't want it to be—but it had entered a new phase. Seeing Marco and Chiara's evident happiness made him happy. He couldn't wait for their next stages, for the weddings and grandchildren, for the Christmases to come.

He was especially grateful at how welcome they had made Rebecca, each one conjuring up a gift for her, just as she had for them. The house had been full of happiness on Christmas morning, not so much for what they received—although Chiara had been clearly emotional when she opened her present to discover her mother's engagement ring and the matching earrings—but because they were together. And now they were seeing in the New Year together, first here at the ballet and then back at the Grand York at the traditional New Year's Eve Ball.

'A box,' Chiara breathed, coming to stand next to him to peer over the ornate rail at the people taking their seats below. 'I feel so fancy.' She might be dating a billionaire but Chiara still had her feet firmly on the ground, delighting in the champagne and canapés served to them at their seats, at the glitter and lights, at the music.

'Me too,' Eleanora agreed, smiling at a small girl in a huge poufy dress clinging onto her mother's hand, eyes wide. 'I vote we add the ballet at Christmas to our family Christmas traditions, Marco.'

'Thanks to Dad, I think that will be very

possible,' Marco agreed. 'Ballet is clearly going to be at the heart of our family from now on. Who knows, maybe that's a dancer we have growing in there.' He lightly touched her stomach and she covered his hand with hers.

'He or she is certainly lively enough.'

They fell silent as the orchestra stopped warming up and the house lights fell, the conductor walked in to applause and the overture started up. Joshua sat back, prepared to be entertained, but in the end he was completely transported: to the party, to the battle between the toy soldiers and the mice, and then to the magic kingdom of snow and sweets. Thanks to Rebecca, he knew the effort that went into making this look effortless: the years of training and dedication of the dancers, the army of seamstresses, make-up artists and hairdressers, the technical staff skilled in every discipline from carpentry to welding to painting, who created the stunning backdrops, the musicians in the pit, making the music come alive as if new, not one of the most beloved scores in history. Not unlike a hotel, all the effort was hidden so those watching saw only the result.

It just made him appreciate her all the more. Rebecca was in charge of all of this.

And he knew how much it meant to her to share it with him and his family.

Rebecca stood backstage in the spot she had stood so many hundreds, thousands, of times it was a surprise there was no outline of her feet imprinted there. From here she had waited to go on as a child in the party scenes, as a member of the corps, her job to blend in in every way, to be part of a whole. Then in a featured role, a soloist and finally as a principal. And now she stood here night after night and watched her dancers create magic.

She had lost count of how many *Nutcrackers* she had watched and danced, but the much-loved ballet never failed to transport her into its wintry wonderland and tonight was no exception. It was almost a shock when Clara woke up and recalled her adventures, the curtains falling to tumultuous applause. The curtain calls went on and on, the audience on their feet as Freya, who had made her debut as the Sugar Plum Fairy that night, led Rebecca out to take her bow.

The years fell away as she stepped under the spotlights. How many times had she, as Freya did tonight, approached the conductor and Artistic Director and led them onto the stage?

But not only was she not in a tutu but a floor-length silvery evening dress, this time there were people in the audience for her and her alone. Not fans, but family. Joshua, Chiara and Evan, Eleanora and Marco were applauding wildly—applauding her. Miraculously, her parents and sisters and their families were also in the audience. Joshua had organised rooms for them at the Grand York and invited them to the New Year's Eve Ball—and they had all accepted. Earlier in the day she had taken the Pearsons and her youngest sister and her family on a backstage tour, delighted in their interest and questions and awe of her everyday world. She was still in awe of it, of the way the combination of light and music and costume and movement could create such emotions.

And she was in awe of how she felt about the man in the box opposite as he stood and clapped, his gaze fixed on her, his smile wide. In awe of his heart, of his achievements, of the family he had raised, of his capacity for happiness, despite everything, for his lack of jealousy and appreciation of her for being her. It made her want to be the best she could be. To be worthy of him. To support him the way he supported her. To love his family as her own. To belong.

Loving him and being loved by him was a privilege and as Rebecca held his gaze she vowed never to forget it.

EPILOGUE

One year later

'YOU'RE HERE!'

'Happy Christmas!'

'We saved you plenty of food.'

'How did the show go?'

Rebecca walked into the cabin late on Christmas Eve to a chorus of greetings and hugs. She stopped just long enough to hang up her coat and remove her shoes before swooping up baby Gabriel and smothering his chubby cheeks in kisses.

'He loves you.' Eleanora smiled at her son as he reached for Rebecca's hair.

'The feeling is mutual,' Rebecca said, squeezing the little boy tight. She had never really known babies before and was enjoying every new stage of Gabriel's babyhood almost as much as his parents and doting grandpa. 'The show went really well, thank you. The audience went home for Christmas happy, and the dancers, crew and musicians all get a much-deserved break for a couple of days. I'm sorry I wasn't here to help decorate the tree, but I appreciate you video calling me while you did it.'

'Of course! Someone had to arbitrate over where the lights went,' Chiara called from the kitchen, where she was heating up the promised food, the beautiful sapphire flashing on her left hand; she and Evan were planning a Bali wedding in a few weeks' time. Rebecca couldn't wait.

She handed Gabriel over to Joshua as she collected her food and took it to the table. She was often happy to be the observer on family occasions, to watch them interact, to enjoy the warm teasing, the affection. To know that she belonged. Tonight was no different as Chiara and Marco began the great tradition of bickering over which Christmas films they would watch, even though the outcome—the same as last year—was a foregone conclusion.

'Happy with the tree?' Joshua placed a glass of wine in front of her before hooking a chair to sit opposite.

'You chose wisely,' she assured him. They had video called her during the tree selection as well, making sure that she didn't miss out on any of the day.

'I'm sorry I didn't come to collect you,' Joshua said, and she smiled at him, affection filling her.

'The car Evan sent was quite adequate. Adequate in terms of absurdly luxurious. So comfortable I almost snoozed. Besides, Grandpa, you were needed here. You don't want to miss a second of Gabriel's induction into the Pearson Family Christmas traditions.'

She wasn't being polite. She had been more than happy to make her own way to the cabin, especially in the chauffeured car Evan had provided. She and Joshua had found their equilibrium early. Joshua had persuaded the Board and Marco to invest in the chain of inns and spent part of each week on the road; the rest of the time he stayed with Rebecca. If he was away longer, he was usually based here in the cabin and she would arrange to work from home for a few days and join him, making sure she downed tools to ski, hike and appreciate the countryside. When apart they spoke every day, both interested in the other's progress and work. She had visited all the inns and was now a frequent visitor to the Grand York Hotel, while Joshua could now identify all the dancers, knew her admin staff by name and came to every first night, no matter what his schedule.

It was all so easy. For the first few months Rebecca hadn't quite trusted just how easy it was, wondering when reality would intrude. It had taken her time to accept that this *was* reality, that she could be this happy and fulfilled in her personal life as well as her work.

She looked over at the family portrait on the wall, Gabriella glowing, with her arms around her small children and, as she always did, sent her a thank you. She never felt jealous of the woman Joshua had loved so deeply, rather she felt that she had Gabriella's blessing.

Joshua took her empty bowl. 'Fancy a walk?'

'And miss the movies?'

'We'll be back for The Muppets.'

Rebecca had been inside all day and the evening, although cold, looked enticing, snow covering the ground, the stars bright in a velvety sky.

'Okay. Let me get ready.'

A few minutes later they were walking around the lake, skirting Anita and Trudie's cabin, this year lit brightly, the sound of voices carrying clearly through the still night. Rebecca had turned down the invitation to the party, knowing she wouldn't arrive until late, but they planned to spend some of Christmas Day with her friends.

She smiled affectionately at the cabin. Grand as it was, she had never felt at home there the way she did at Joshua's, but she was very grateful for the sanctuary and new start it had given her—and to the friends whose generosity had made both possible.

They walked a little way hand in hand, Joshua unusually quiet, until they came to a natural glade by the water's edge. Rebecca stopped and looked up at the night sky, breathing in the cold, the freshness of the air, the atmosphere. 'It's so beautiful here,' she said.

'It is.' But he wasn't looking at the sky, he was looking at her.

'I wanted to give you a present early,' he said, looking uncharacteristically nervous.

'Oh?' Her heart started to beat faster, his solemnity breaking the spell of the night sky.

'Rebecca.' He stopped, swallowed. 'Rebecca, I love you.'

'I know.' And she did know, and she would never stop being grateful for the miracle that had brought him into her life. 'I love you too.' The words were so easy to say, in a way they had never been before.

'And I want to spend the rest of my life with you.' To her shock, he dropped to one knee, holding out a small turquoise box. 'Rebecca Nelson. Will you do me the greatest of honours and marry me?'

'Get up, it's freezing! Yes, of course yes.' She pulled him up, laughing and crying all at once, reaching up to pull his head to hers, kissing him with all the love and happiness filling her.

'Are you sure? I come with two children and a very noisy grandson...'

'And I wouldn't want you any other way.'

'You haven't looked at the ring yet. You might change your mind when you see it.'

She held up her gloved hand. 'Not the most practical attire for ring boxes.' She pulled the glove off, too excited to feel the cold, and took the box, opening it to see a beautiful platinum ring, studded with small diamonds.

'It's an eternity ring,' he said. 'This is a second chance for both of us. I want you to know what that means to me. But if you want something more traditional, we can go pick it out when we get back to the city.'

'No, no, I love it. Thank you.' She did. It was elegantly beautiful, unostentatious, perfect. She held out her hand. 'Quick, put it on before I get frostbite! It seems a shame to cover it back up though.' She watched breathlessly as he slid the ring onto her fourth finger, and then she slipped her hand back into the glove. She kissed him again, breathing him in, loving the solidity of him, his warmth and steadiness, his strong moral compass, his capability. His heart.

'I thought last Christmas was the best Christmas ever,' she told him, cupping his face in her gloved hands and drinking in the familiar sight of him, the dark brown eyes, salt and pepper hair, laughing mouth, features that made her stomach twist with desire, her heart beat faster with love, her whole body relax, knowing she was safe. 'Looks like I spoke too soon.'

'Here's to a lifetime of Christmases together,' he said as he kissed her again.

'I can't wait.' She meant every word. Her life with Joshua was an adventure, one she relished every second of—and as she leaned into his kiss she knew the best was yet to come.

* * * * *

If you missed the previous stories in the
A Five-Star Family Reunion trilogy
check out

Wearing His Ring til Christmas
by Nina Singh
and
One-Night Baby to Christmas Proposal
by Susan Meier

And, if you enjoyed this story,
check out these other great reads
from Jessica Gilmore

The Princess and the Single Dad
Cinderella and the Vicomte
Winning Back His Runaway Bride

All available now!